Enchantments And Dragons

Mary Catelli

Published by Wizard's Wood Press, 2015.

This is a work of fiction. Similarities to real people, places, or events are entirely coincidental.

ENCHANTMENTS AND DRAGONS

First edition. January 1, 2015.

Written by Mary Catelli.

The Manor, the Maze, and the Unicorn

Cecily pushed through the rosebushes. Branches and red roses prodded from either side, reaching for her carefully put-up hair and for the skirts of a gown she wore for travel and here, where her clothing did not matter, but they did not catch her. She reached the stone bench, where the servants, who did not like the maze, would not see her, as they might anywhere else. There, she took out her mother's letter. For a minute, while it lay in her lap, she fought for calm. Before she broke the seal, she could dream of its contents.

Her fingers tightened until the paper crinkled. Queen Blanche of Ankelia regarded Clearwater as a manor to send the disgraced to—for their health, when her own health had grown worse than that of any courtier she had ever sent here.

Her parents knew that.

They also knew that the queen's agents read her letters.

Cecily noted how well they had restored the seal. She broke it.

"To my beloved daughter, Cecily, greetings.

"Your lord father and I were gladdened by the honor, that the queen had sent you to her own castle—"

Cecily stopped reading. Even great nobles could not thwart the queen, and her parents were not great. Her finger itched. Only her weariness with Clearwater had brought about even fancies of escape that way.

She forced her breath out. Some victims of Queen Blanche's disfavor had left here, in time; she had to keep her wits about her.

She scanned the rest of what her mother wrote. She thought her mother knew the truth. Writing to her, Cecily had said only that Queen Blanche had sent her to Clearwater, not that when she had asked to leave her post and marry Sir Alain, Queen Blanche had broken her finger in rage. A bee, brightly gold, buzzed over the deep red rose before her, and she watched its flight. She had known when she asked that the never-married queen did not like her ladies to marry—whatever she said about not interfering with any honest match—but Queen Blanche had never raged so before. Least of all for a minor lady-in-waiting. Even the elderly ladies who had tutted over her rashness in asking had been surprised by the queen, though they did not admit it.

The letter fluttered into her lap. Weeks had not helped. Cecily's heart ached. Now, she knew what Alain was like. He had turned green at the prospect of opposing the queen's wishes.

"The coward," Cecily whispered. The vile, odious, faithless coward—who still lived at court. While the queen consigned her here.

Cecily stood and slid the letter back in her sleeve. She could wander the maze for her amusement. She would not let her confinement drive her mad. Perhaps she might even learn a truth or two about the tales of Clearwater.

Before her, a rosebush bore small white flowers, so thickly that she could barely see any green. Their scent burdened the air, and the greenery half hid a gate. Cecily had not realized she had come so far, but she reached for the latch.

The woods stood far off to her right. Before her, down a slope, the village stood, surrounded by field and pasture. Children played about the cottages, and chickens pecked. On one threshold, a woman spun. A small girl scurried up and buried her face in the woman's lap. The woman stroked her hair. Cecily, sick with envy, looked away.

That was when she saw a company on the road, with fore riders and men in livery, and fine blooded traveling horses.

Her mouth went dry.

She tried to calm herself. Messengers had come before—but a messenger was a single rider. Someone else had fallen from favor, someone whom she could speak with.

Or perhaps—no, Queen Blanche would not send an invalid here. This person, out of favor, could not help her escape.

That did not squelch the spring of hope.

Half the servants wore the queen's livery, but the other half rode clad in green and silver. Cecily racked her memory. Their banner rippled, enough to show a white stag on green.

The morning was warm, but Cecily felt frozen. A bee buzzed about her. The livery of Norland, of King David—an ambassador. Queen Blanche might have sent him here for his health. She forced her breath out. More likely, to keep him from pressing his master's cause.

When he came from Queen Blanche's nephew? The heir to Ankelia's throne? What had the queen *thought*?

"I should greet him," she whispered.

She walked back, through brambles heavy with red and golden flowers. Petals fell about her like rain, and she swept them from her hair and gown. She reached the courtyard gate as hooves clattered on the cobblestones. In the midst of the company, a horse bore a man with silvery hair and beard. He dressed too finely to be anyone but the ambassador: his mantle was fur-lined, and rings glinted on his fingers. Two liveried men came to help him dismount. His eyes closed, he held their arms after his feet were planted.

Cecily blinked, realizing that he might be ill. After a moment biting her lip, she pondered how ill health was no guarantee of the queen's favor.

He opened his eyes and looked at her. She flinched and wondered if she had brushed off all the petals, but entered the courtyard to curtsey.

"My lord? Did the Queen's Grace speak of my presence at Clearwater? I am Cecily, a lady-in-waiting here to—" She hesitated. What Queen Blanche had said she suffered *from*?

"You must forgive me, Lady Cecily. My illness—I grow absent-minded. I am Stephan of Blakmere." The ambassador managed a sketchy bow. Cecily wondered whether it was Lord Stephan or Sir Stephan, but he looked pale.

"My lord, you are ill, you must rest—" She turned to the castellan. "My chamber was ready when I arrived. King David's ambassador is worthy of greater attention."

The castellan puffed up, opened his mouth as if to rebuke her, and collapsed. The few advantages of being a high-born lady here—she did not smile.

"This way, Lord Stephan," he said. Lord Stephan and half a dozen of the company followed.

A dark, thin young man looked at the untended garden, and said, "What a place to send an ambassador."

It is good for your health, thought Cecily. However much the courtiers or even the queen detest you, they find it hard to remember you while you are here.

Sunlight threw vast, dusty sunbeams down the hallway. Cecily inched along it, her footsteps faintly echoing. A gentlewoman might call on an old and ailing gentleman. Especially as the dark young man—his secretary Philip, the servants said—had admitted, after Mass, that Lord Stephan would welcome her.

Even if the servants whispered that both the ambassador and his secretary were unmarried, and given her sly glances. As if losing Alain had made her eager to lose her heart again. As if she still did not need the queen's leave to marry.

But it would be kindly on her part to visit him. The manor had little for anyone to do. An invalid would find it worse than she did. And, at that, she did not know whether he would write letters to anyone, and mention her with favor.

The servants' tongues had wagged about her since she had arrived, and most likely before. This visit would not change that.

She reached the door, its wood dark in the whitewashed hall. Cecily knocked.

Philip opened it. He looked at her without his impassive face moving at all, but called, "Lady Cecily came to call."

"A gracious gesture to an old man," said Lord Stephan, firmly enough. Cecily edged inside, through the antechamber. In the bedchamber, he sat in a high-backed chair, with his feet on a stool. Smiling, he gestured at another chair.

She folded her hands in her lap there. "I hope you will find my conversation pleasing. Despite my name, I fear that I neither sing nor play an instrument well."

"A bright-eyed lady always brings cheer to a sickroom."

Even here, an ambassador. Cecily spoke slowly, to choose her words with care. "To fall ill in foreign lands, far from your family—it must be harder than at home, where the feminine company is easier to come by."

"Mostly, my lady—but then, I never married, and so even in my home country. . . ." Lord Stephan shook his head.

"When you have time to visit your brother," said Philip, "Mother and my sisters make you welcome."

Cecily blinked.

Lord Stephan laughed. "Lady Cecily, I give you Philip, my secretary and nephew, my brother's youngest. For fear of his mother, he has no mercy on me."

Philip turned his face away.

"Though I spent little time there, for much the same reason as I never wed: too much time in the king's service. Not that I begrudge him it. A treaty is a fine legacy —if only the peace it brings. . . ." He shivered. How ill was he? Cecily wondered, but he found his voice again. "You young folk do not wish to listen to an old man's ramblings."

"Oh, no, please my lord," said Cecily. Philip joined her in pressing him, and life returned to his face as Lord Stephan spoke again of his work for the king.

When he fell silent again, Cecily asked about the court.

"Little is happening, my lady," said Lord Stephan. "His Majesty, the King of Iltria, sent an embassy, but it brought only festivities and flowery speeches."

Philip snorted. "If it is merely festivities. Iltrians do nothing without an ulterior motive. Great plotters, them."

"One can plot one's way into a queen's good graces," said Lord Stephan, "in case one needs it one day."

Cecily smiled wryly. If the Iltrians thought to win Queen Blanche's good will, their reputation as plotters lacked merit. "The courtiers must enjoy the festivities." The queen must enjoy the flattery, but a lady-in-waiting could not say that, even this far from the queen.

"Your blooming health will soon restore you to such festivities," said Lord Stephan.

Cecily managed a smile, but her finger itched. Odd that the queen would send him here, when he actually was ill, but still odder that no one had warned him that her health had not caused her presence.

Philip shifted his weight and cast Cecily a sideways glance. "I doubt it."

"Come, nephew—you didn't listen to the tales that people are sent here as punishment?" Cecily stiffened, and Lord Stephan went on. "Your castellan here, Master Rod—"

"Master Roderick," said Cecily.

"Was this a punishment for him?"

"No," said Cecily, "his father served the queen, went on embassies—took a foreign bride, even. The Queen's Grace gave him this post to support himself and his widowed mother."

"Then again," said Lord Stephan, "for you. . . ."

In the silence, Philip said, "Peasants talked of creatures in the woods."

"So they say." Cecily hunted for tales, as a mild and innocuous matter. If she wandered through the gardens later, perhaps she would have a tale of her own to amuse them with.

By the forest, white roses grew wild. Cecily meandered in the shade, beneath white birches and sweet-smelling pines, careful to never lose sight of the maze, until she grew tired and leaned against a pine. This last week had been less dull, but Lord Stephan needed rest. Wandering the maze filled some hours.

She looked up. Pine needles formed a green roof. Queen Blanche could have had Lord Stephan attended by her best physicians at court.

Queen Blanche never let her rages interfere with affairs of state, before. Then, she had never broken a lady-in-waiting's finger, before, either. Cecily pushed on the rough bark to stand straight again.

Something white moved among the trees. Cecily blinked, but it was not that the birch branch had shifted in the wind. In the shadows stood a unicorn, whiter than any birch. She gasped.

As small as a goat and daintier, the unicorn moved from the pines and birches into the darker shade of the oaks. She did not think it had seen her; she caught her breath and stared. It seemed to gleam in the shadows—its thick mane pale gold, its sharp horn a richer shade of gold. It nibbled on the leaves of an oak sapling and vanished among the trees.

Cecily drew in a long breath. A breeze touched her, reminding her that noon, and the heat, approached. She walked toward the castle, only glancing back six or seven times, and feeling no surprise that it had not returned. No wonder the waters here were clear and wholesome, with a unicorn to purify them. And an impish thought said it was no wonder that poachers were so scarce, when only a maiden would be safe in the woods. That golden horn could be dangerous.

She could tell Lord Stephan and Philip about the unicorn— but no. To prattle about such a creature? —and she could not show them the unicorn, not without endangering them. Whatever their moral character, the unicorn only favored female virgins.

In the antechamber, Philip worked on letters and only nodded to her. As his pen scratched across the paper, Cecily walked into the master chamber. Lord Stephan sat by the window, but his shoulders were hunched, and a blanket covered his lap. Cecily let her breath out. A week, and he worsened.

Lord Stephan looked up. His face eased. "It is good of you to come listen to an ailing old man ramble, my lady."

"It is kind of you to amuse a foolish maiden, my lord."

"Foolish?" Lord Stephan arched an eyebrow.

"All maidens are foolish, I learned at court. It spares courtiers difficulty of telling one from another."

Lord Stephan laughed and had difficulty regaining his breath. Cecily sat, watching him. She remembered the unicorn, her thoughts turned to poison, and then she could no longer hear Lord Stephan. She only vaguely heard that he spoke.

Her tongue touched her lips. Poison would explain why no one else ailed, why Lord Stephan did not recover—but if he suffered from poison, there were only King David's men at Clearwater, and Queen Blanche's.

It might be a spy, Cecily thought stoutly.

Lord Stephan's eyebrows went up. "My lady? Was your walk so dreadful you could not bear to speak of it?"

Her face burned. "I must beg your pardon. I. . . ." She shrank from confessing the truth and hearing them laugh at it—"My mother says that feeding the ill matters greatly. I should oversee your diet."

Lord Stephan leaned back.

"I should see to that now and return when I am fit company, with my wits about me."

Lord Stephan smiled, as if at a child's whim.

Philip stood in the doorway. "Queen Blanche sends ailing courtiers to Clearwater. The cooks are accustomed to the ill."

Cecily rose. "No care is too great for your uncle."

"Let Lady Cecily reassure herself, Philip," said Lord Stephan. "Women like to be useful."

Her heart pounded in her chest, not more rapidly than usual, but harder. She held her tongue. To tell them that she feared poison—she had no name to give them—and any poisoner would learn of the charge swiftly if either of them ever spoke of a word of it where a servant could hear. She tried to keep her smile innocuous. She had not thought she could prove useful here, but she would not flinch from it.

Philip moved from her way, but slowly.

The sullen fire in the great fireplace was not enough to light the kitchen, but it was enough to heat it —especially in midsummer. Most of the servants were half-naked, and Cecily's hair stuck to her neck. She did not budge.

"I know how to cook," the cook said.

"I must oversee it," said Cecily. "Even a spice may cause harm to the ailing."

Servants grimaced. She could not judge whether they all were only annoyed with her, or whether some had been foiled.

"Lord Stephan has eaten your food a week," Cecily said. "He still ails. Indeed, he sickens further. It would be a disgrace if I did not to all that I could to aid the ambassador to our queen."

The cook grumbled under her breath. Potboys and kitchen maids retreated to their work. Cecily stood by the door, where she could watch their work, and where it was a little cooler.

The cook mixed up the pastry from the finest, whitest floor, and the fruit compote, and the milk pudding, with port to fortify. Cecily watched the ingredients as servants brought them from the pantry, and the dishes as they slowly cooked.

"Fitting, my lady?" said the cook, with a sneer.

"I will assure my lord that I have overseen it. In the morning, I will return for Lord Stephan's breakfast." She reached for the tray and carried it into the courtyard.

"My lady!" Philip's voice rang as he came toward her. "After your kindness—to make you *carry* it."

A thought half-formed in Cecily's head. "It was my pleasure," she said.

In the gray morning light, the courtyard stones were wet with dew. The castellan waited in the kitchen's doorway. The cook lurked behind him, as he sputtered, "Most improper—can not permit—Queen Blanche commended you to my care!"

"It is clear, Master Roderick," said Cecily, "*you* have not gone to court. A lady properly oversees the kitchen and tends the sick. Furthermore, it would insult King David to offer Lord Stephan less than the best care." She brushed by the castellan, into the kitchen, where servants readied a breakfast. She snatched fruit from the hands of kitchen maids and hurled them into the fire. While castellan and servants gaped, she upended porridge after them.

"Begin again," she said, sweetly. "While I watch."

For the weeks, the heat grew, broken only now and again by thunderstorms. Every so often, Cecily thought that Lord Stephan regained color and slept less; then, that she fooled herself. At church, she prayed for patience.

Then, one morning as he ate, Lord Stephan said, "A splendid day. Perhaps I should enjoy the gardens—for the air."

Cecily's heart seemed to stop, and then it hammered. She feared hope, and could not squelch it.

"If you tire—" said Philip.

"After Lady Cecily's good care?" Lord Stephan smiled. "Servants enough to help me, if I am so foolish."

For a moment, Cecily thought Philip would weep with relief.

A grassy square, with stone benches, was bordered with bushes. Philip stood with his hands on his hips. A bush bore fiery orange roses before him, and the still, warm air was burdened with the sweetness of their scent. "How far do these roses range?"

"Philip, Philip," said Lord Stephan, though his gaze surveyed the square before them, "Lady Cecily has only stayed here three months. How can you expect her to have wandered through all the labyrinth?"

"It is hard to judge how much I have seen," said Cecily. "With a garden this size, and it a labyrinth to boot."

Lord Stephan smiled. "I think that I will not try to see more, today." Philip helped him to the bench. Cecily hesitated, wondering whether to sit herself.

"How often do royal messengers arrive here, Lady Cecily?" Lord Stephan asked.

Cecily blinked. "When there is a message," she said mildly, sitting on another bench. A bee buzzed over her skirt, and she sat very still, waiting for it to discern the cloth was not a flower. "Perhaps once or twice a month—peasants can bear a message to town, for a messenger, though you may have to wait until one goes to sell mushrooms or watercress. I wrote to my parents so."

"I thought so," Lord Stephan said, as if musing. "Do you know much of the succession, Lady Cecily?"

Philip moved sharply but said nothing.

Cecily crossed her ankles and folded her hands in her lap. She wanted to hear this no more than Philip wanted her to, but her mother had drilled her in the succession before even considering letting her attend the queen—and she had learned little more since then.

"The Queen's Grace," she said, unable to keep from sounding prim, "does not seek counsel among her ladies-in-waiting."

Philip snorted. "Better than some places she's sought it." He put one foot on a bench and leaned forward, intent.

"Certain kingdoms wish to—alter it," said Lord Stephan. "The Queen's Grace seems to favor them." He sighed, as if thinking on how futile talk was, this far from the queen. "I sent word to the King's Grace—"

Philip's voice broke in. "What is that?" He climbed on a bench to peer over the maze walls. "Someone's coming."

Her heart pattering, Cecily climbed herself; lacking Philip's inches, she stretched on her toes. She wobbled and felt a hand on her arm. She glanced sideways at Philip, and her face felt hot, but she took advantage of his arm to look.

"It's—a messenger," she said. "They come often enough, for the castellan."

"Perhaps he sent one," said Lord Stephan. "Telling of your health, and how you can return to court. The young gentlemen at court would amuse you better than one sick old man, and a young man bent on nursing him."

Cecily looked down and felt mulish. The young gentlemen who had not cared when the queen sent her to Clearwater? Not even enough to wish her a safe journey?

By the window, Cecily combed out her hair. In the morning gray, the messenger readied himself to leave—before even she went to the kitchen for Lord Stephan's breakfast.

Someone moved from the maze. Cecily lowered her comb. Philip walked from the roses to the messenger and spoke. Her mouth pursed, and she went back to combing. Philip *had* written letters. He would want them dispatched, and he might not have another chance for a month.

Her comb caught a tangle, and she lifted it to carefully tease it out. A cold thought came up: If Philip were Lord Stephan's nephew, he might also be his heir.

The sunset blazed in deep crimson and purple, and below the courtyard's cobbles were swathed in the darkness, but the air still steamed. Cecily walked to the kitchen door, where sullen orange light seeped out from the fires, and the heat hit like a further blow.

"Good evening, my lady," said the cook. Cecily looked about. The dark kitchen seemed sibilant with excitement, with servants casting sidelong glances.

She studied their faces, orange and black in the gloom, with the oddly cast shadows making them look like gargoyles. She had no reason to believe that anything had changed.

Any more than she had had, at first, to suspect poison.

She nodded to them and went to watch their handiwork. They made only dishes she had seen them prepare before, and she saw nothing untoward about their work.

The chamber held only two candles, which added more heat even than was pleasant—the open windows offered only faint coolness from occasional breezes—but though they left most of the room in shadow, they glowed golden on the table and the dishes there.

As he ate, Lord Stephan said, "Perhaps, Lady Cecily, you and Philip might amuse yourself with a game of draughts?"

It would pass the hours, thought Cecily. And who could sleep when the heat lingered so?

But while they played, the shadows of the pieces crossing the board—before the game had gotten well started—Lord Stephan made a strange noise. His tray rattled against the table, as if he did not have the strength to put it there.

Philip leapt up, knocking the game awry. Her lap filled with pieces, Cecily stared at the new lines on Lord Stephan's face. She could not have moved. The food had held poison. Under her gaze, they had poisoned the food.

Cecily closed her eyes and swallowed. If she had not seen them in the kitchen, she might have fooled herself into thinking that he had never been poisoned, she had been a fool, and this was just a relapse of his illness, but—she had.

Her hands formed fists and released them again. Every servant in the kitchen was party to the poisoning. Queen Blanche had to know that.

A noise made her open her eyes. Philip brought his uncle toward the bed. She forced out a deep breath. She had seen him meet the messenger—though she felt guilty, when he leaned so anxiously over his uncle.

Cecily put the pieces back on the table, each one clicking against the wood. She wrestled with her thoughts: the queasy feeling that it was possible; a cold nausea that declared that *Philip* would not, that he loved his uncle; an odd hope that Queen Blanche would not be offended. . . .

The last piece clicked on the table from her fingers, and she looked at them, and the shadows they cast. She did not even know that the food held poison. Only the unicorn's presence had suggested it to her.

Then another thought struck her.

Philip had been so anxious that he agreed to not feed Lord Stephan until she returned—or deceived her to perfection.

Cecily glared at the towering oaks. They made her feel even smaller than she had felt before, and their boughs spread leaves over every inch, muffling both sky and sun, leaving her in shadow. She eyed the ground again: thick dead leaves showed no hoof prints. She could not wander too far into the forest, or she would never find her way out again, unicorn or no unicorn. The leaves showed her footprints no better than they did the unicorn's hooves.

The air hung still about her, already heated this early in the morning. She walked on. Lord Stephan might die without it. Even if she were wicked enough to watch in silence, he was a royal ambassador. Wars had started over less.

The still air had not changed, but Cecily stopped, feeling chilled. If Queen Blanche had connived at the poison, Cecily was defying her, and in more than her desire to marry. Her breath came rapid and shallow, and she fixed her gaze on the forest floor, trying not to trip. If King David had displeased her, Queen Blanche could name a different heir. She had no need to murder the messenger.

A root nearly sent her sprawling. She grabbed a tree, to steady herself. Innocence would not help *her*. If Queen Blanche decided she should stay in Clearwater, she would rot there.

That thought would not leave her.

Cecily shook her head, and ran.

She burst into a fern-laden gap, where a fallen tree had opened the forest floor to the sun. Plants there showed signs of nibbles. Perhaps it was not the unicorn, but she found tracks and ran after them. Acorns lay underfoot, rolling when she stepped on one, but she could not stop.

She came about an oak, like every other in the grove, and nearly collided with the unicorn. A wildflower hanging from its mouth, it looked at her with dark eyes. Cecily stared. Its head came little higher than her waist, and its horn could barely reach her shoulder.

The unicorn tossed its head, catching the rest of the flower in its mouth.

I hope it's not hungry, thought Cecily, but the gardens held roses and grass. She took up her rope. The unicorn eyed it inquisitively. Cecily stepped closer. The unicorn sniffed at the air and pressed closer. The horn passed inches from her arm, and her mouth went dry at its sharpness, but the unicorn pressed its head to her side. Cecily eased the rope about its neck. Its expression was one of bright-eyed wonder, and when Cecily tugged on the rope, the unicorn gamboled alongside.

When the roses appeared ahead, the unicorn cocked its ears and pressed against the rope. Cecily hurried to keep up as it cavorted into the gardens, nibbling on this rose and that.

Having no wish to carry the food through the entire maze, Cecily tugged on the rope. The unicorn took a mouthful of red roses and munched as they walked. No sooner had it finished the red roses than it tugged against the rope to get at a bush laden with yellow ones. Cecily tried to pull back, but the unicorn did not stir without a mouthful of those flowers. Then it turned away, giving her an innocent look as it chomped.

We are getting closer, Cecily told herself, just slowly. She led the unicorn on, considering. Not too close to the castle. She did not want to endanger everyone there, and the maze held out-of-the-way courtyards where a unicorn could merrily nibble on roses.

Philip stood by the manor door. He looked as haggard as Lord Stephan had. "He's very ill. He needs to eat."

"Did the servants bring up food?" said Cecily

"Without your overseeing them? Yes."

Cecily nodded. "Give me it then."

Philip took a step backwards, as if to get a better look at her. "The tray's heavy."

Cecily considered the weight, what the unicorn might do if someone else carried it, that the unicorn would prove that she knew of poison. "I will carry it myself, nevertheless." She held out her hands. I can not explain, she thought. Even to tell why I can not explain. That would explain that I do not trust you.

Her arms aching, Cecily laid the tray on the bench and undid the latch. She still had to carry it back. Next time, Philip could carry the tray closer.

She picked the tray up and pushed the gate farther open, with her hip, to enter the courtyard. The unicorn was not on the grass, it was not nibbling at the bushes, it was not drinking from the fountain—her heart seemed to stop. She picked out the rope. Though still tied to the bench, it did not raise her hopes. She followed its path through the grass, and where it snaked into the fountain, among the carved dolphins. She walked over. The unicorn looked at her. Perched high on the fountain, invisible from the gate, it bit off roses from a bush, higher than her head, let alone its.

Cecily smiled at its mischievous look. Then its gaze went to the tray she held, and something rippled through it. It clambered down, still delicate, but it looked angry. Its horn glittered in the sunlight.

Cecily, carefully, and keeping her gaze on that sharp horn, lowered the tray on the ground. And stepped back, pulling her skirt away.

The unicorn stepped up, without a glance at her, as if it were picking its way through a foul swamp. It stood over the tray, and its horn went down to touch each dish. Cecily saw no change, in either the horn or the food, but the unicorn gamboled away.

Every dish, thought Cecily, as she went to take the tray up again.

The breakfast tray was lighter than the dinner one had been, but it still weighed on Cecily's arms. She scowled at the gray mist wreathing through the garden. Lord Stephan was sicker than he had been before. Their one dose must had been greater than before.

The gate appeared, and she shifted the tray to open it. Inside, most of the roses had vanished—everywhere within the unicorn's reach—and it innocently nibbled at the rope.

Cecily's tongue touched her lips. The gate would keep the unicorn within—unless it ate through the metal. It looked like a goat. Perhaps it ate like one, too.

Its expression turned fierce at the sight of the breakfast. Cecily lowered the food and pondered. She would move it about the gardens, to fresh rosebushes—and use a longer rope.

At least with Philip so anxious, and Lord Stephan so sick, she would have time to watch over it.

By the kitchen, Philip took the tray, and Cecily walked into the garden with him. Servants peered from windows. Her heart pattering faster, Cecily dodged a thorny branch and held it back for Philip.

"We're close, aren't we?" said Philip. He looked at a rosebush. All of its flowers and most of its leaves had been nibbled away. Cecily felt her face heat. She should have paid attention.

"Yes, we are close enough." She held out her hands.

His hands tightened on the tray. "A secret?"

Cecily thought of the unicorn, thought of telling him, remembered her suspicions—and considered that what he did not know, he could not tell. "Let your uncle tell you: women like to keep secrets as well as to feel useful."

His mouth twisted. He handed over the tray.

Roses hid him from view swiftly, and she hurried past hedges and a gate, to where the unicorn idly ate the grass down to the dirt.

Cecily sighed and lowered the tray. The unicorn went on nibbling. She blinked. Minutes later, the unicorn ambled over. It sniffed at the dishes and chomped on a pastry.

She yanked the tray up, not quickly enough to save that pastry from the unicorn. It munched it down.

Cecily let her breath out. The unicorn was, she supposed, entitled to some reward. She looked at the dishes. If they had learned she was undoing their poison, they might well stop it, but she could not. Only by returning with every meal could she ensure that it ceased forever.

Evening breezes stirred the candlelight. Cecily stood by the window, feeling restless. Lord Stephan's face was still lined with pain.

A week, she thought. After a single dose of poison. For a moment she closed her eyes and wondered why she was not wringing her hands.

Philip eased him into the chair. At least, Lord Stephan accepted his nephew's aid. It would be a disgrace if he were, with Philip so devoted to—

Cecily felt the breeze as if it were ice. He seemed devoted him to his uncle, but she *had* realized he could have every reason to act, and then neglected that knowledge.

She let out her breath in a rush. She could not mistrust Philip forever. On the morrow, when he carried the tray for her, she would invent some excuse to leave. He would be alone with his uncle. One way or another, she would know.

And then, and then—she supposed Queen Blanche might be grateful to hear of such treachery.

The thought did not stir even a fugitive flicker of hope.

They came out of the roses, where dew still lay heavy on every leaf, and the doorway stood ahead of them. Cecily glanced at the windows. She could see no one. She had to. . . .

She saw a flutter in one window. "That's Meg. I must speak with her."

Philip blinked.

"Give Lord Stephan my regrets." She grabbed the latch. She could not tell him why she had to go, she had not thought up an excuse, but she had committed herself. She might never have another chance.

Within the dim hallway, she fled. Her footsteps echoed, but all else was silence; Philip neither followed her nor climbed the stairs. She could almost feel his gaze.

Cecily darted about a corner. She forced herself to breathe deeply. She had to give Philip time to reach the room, to— poison the meal, to give his uncle the food. *Then* she could see if Lord Stephan sickened again.

It would break his heart, she thought. It might kill him faster than the poison. . . .

She walked, and walked, and could not out-walk her thoughts, and was glad that she met no servants. Down a hall, around the back way where roses grew over the windows and filtered the morning light to greenness, and up the back stairs. She felt ill as she walked down the last hall.

The room lay in sunlight. She opened the door too softly to disturb them. Lord Stephan offered a dish to Philip. He ate some. Cecily felt almost dizzy.

"Lady Cecily!" Lord Stephan said. "Philip said that you had to run off."

"I had to speak with a servant," Cecily said. "With—a woman servant."

Philip looked at the food in his hand. Cecily felt her heart sink.

The morning had yet to melt away the mist, and dew lay thick on the grass. Cecily told herself that, overwrought, she had imagined Philip's glance. It was as foolish as fancying that he had tried to poison his uncle.

Philip's voice came from behind, low but carrying. "That was a test."

She flinched.

"You gave me the chance to poison my uncle."

Cecily found that her tongue would not move, but her ears heard everything. His soft footsteps brought him closer.

"Wasn't it?"

Cecily managed to move her tongue. "Yes, it was a test."

Philip bowed, deeply. "I am in your debt." He smiled. "It shows that you are not party to it yourself."

Cecily let her breath out. She had not thought of that. He had had no more reason to trust her, and—she looked at him. For all his smiles, this was no jest. "They mean to murder Lord Stephan. Subtly if they can. If not—"

"Not at all, if a lady-in-waiting interferes," said Philip.

Lady-in-waiting. Cecily managed a feeble smile. Queen Blanche must have connived at the poisoning. She might wait at Clearwater a long time.

Philip bowed again—to reach her hand, and kiss it. Cecily stood, silent. A courtesy, she told herself. Many men kissed your hand at court.

Then, you were not fool enough to feel the kiss on your hand moments later.

"It's a unicorn," she told him. "I have it captive in the maze."

Her sewing sprawled over her lap, Cecily sat in the shade. Lord Stephan sat across the pool from her, also in the shade. Feeding him sound food for a fortnight merely let him recover, somewhat, and Lord Stephan was not young.

The gate flew open. Philip, a letter in hand, stalked in. "The messenger arrived. The Iltrian ambassador *was* negotiating."

Cecily, feeling invisible, snatched her sewing. "My lords?" Philip looked at her. Her voice grew more timid. "I do not wish to intrude—"

"Oh, stay, stay," snarled Philip. He threw down the paper on the table. "You will hear soon enough. The Iltrian king proposed a match between his youngest son and Lady Eleanor."

Queen Blanche's second cousin. Cecily said, "The King's Grace thinks it suitable?"

Philip laughed. "Queen Blanche has not declared Lady Eleanor her heir without the betrothal in hand."

Iltria! Cecily's sewing fell in her lap. The land was more prosperous than both Ankelia and Norland but lay at such a distance as to make its alliance less valuable—and the alliance would be mutual. Iltria's wars were legion. She looked between Philip and Lord Stephan and wondered what it would mean for Norland.

"I should return to court," said Lord Stephan.

Cecily said, "You are not well enough."

"I knew that King David's service might be the death of me when I entered it. I could have drowned any time I took to the seas." He rose. "Queen Blanche has heeded me before."

Cecily's stomach curdled. The proposed alliance was flattering. Two generations ago, Iltria would never have proposed such a match to Ankelia. Cecily wondered what would befall a plain-speaker who deprived Queen Blanche of the flowery speeches—and for an invalid, in this heat, the journey would be hard. "You have not defied her invitations before."

His eyes narrowed. "I will give myself another week to recover, but not one day more."

Cecily woke early. The sky outside was still black. She sighed and stared at her bed's canopy. Tomorrow, she would not need to rise for Lord Stephan's breakfast, and would have no amusement except her sewing and the labyrinth.

If Lord Stephan hoped to avert the alliance, he could not concern himself with a mere lady-in-waiting, but that stout judgment did not restore her energy. She would think him a fool to risk it when so much evil could result, but she would, once again, be alone without another soul even close to her station.

The morning turned gray. A clatter sounded in the courtyard—a single horse. She rolled over. A messenger, but not one to summon her back to court.

Under the clouding sky, the morning grew darker rather than lighter. In the gloom, roses glowed white, like ghosts, and every now and again, a distant thunder rumbled.

Philip emerged from the manor. "I beg your pardon, Lady Cecily. The castellan spoke—"

Dim though the morning was, Cecily stopped. "You're ill."

Philip froze, as if caught at something. "Nothing much." He took the tray from her hands.

A messenger, thought Cecily. What message? That they had to murder Lord Stephan quickly? That it mattered little if his nephew died with him?

For Philip's sake, Cecily walked slowly. If he were poisoned, he, too, would need to rest. Her mouth felt dry. If she could save them. If not, both Philip and Lord Stephan would sleep well indeed.

She opened a gate and studied his face. If she had not seen the marks on Lord Stephan's face, she would never had realized the subtle ones on Philip's. She bit her lip. It could not be the food. Philip had been well last night, and had not eaten since then.

Trying to think, she drew a deep breath. Dew had damped the air, but she could smell the roses still, and the wetness had stirred up the scent of the earth. . . .

She cursed herself for a fool. The air. They had tainted the chamber's air. She would open the windows—but airing it out do nothing, if they slept in foulness, every night.

And if they ailed, neither Philip nor his uncle could go elsewhere to sleep.

The master chamber felt foul as she walked in. Cecily could not have put a finger on it: the air seemed a little darker and held a scent so light that often she smelled nothing.

She brooded by the open window. Lord Stephan ate, feebly. Perhaps she was even a fool to sit here.

The spoon clattered on the tray. Cecily rose. "I will—Lord Stephan must rest."

Lord Stephan did not stir.

Cecily drew a deep breath. The air was wet with the approaching storm, and smelled faintly of roses. The sky grew darker, but it might not rain.

What if it did rain? She had no need to spare her finery for court—as if what she wore was finery—and she could wander the labyrinth and avoid the maze inside the manor. She left the room, shutting the door softly, so no noise would disturb the patient.

One thing was clear, she thought as she walked the dim corridor. Aiding Lord Stephan would not restore her to court.

I do not *want* to return to court, Cecily thought. Her defiance restored her spirits enough for her to go on. The sky darkened even as she walked, and clouds gathered into great towers of gray.

At the stair's bottom, a small woman waited and curtseyed. "Lady Cecily? The castellan said you must avoid Lord Stephen." She smiled, a thing as superficial as the sheen on an apple. "For fear of—contagion."

Puts *me* in my place, thought Cecily. In her haughtiest voice, she said, "*I* am walking in the garden."

The woman gave the thunderheads a dubious glance, but when Cecily strode ahead, the woman followed.

I wonder if I can lose her, thought Cecily in malice. Then, as white flowers engulfed her, she considered it in earnest. The unicorn might endanger the woman—and if not, the woman could endanger the unicorn. No poisoner would want a unicorn about.

Cecily bit her lip. Perhaps she should restore the unicorn to the forest. She had no need for *it* to suffer.

In the distance, the clouds rumbled louder than ever before.

The woman scrambled after Cecily and looked distressed. "They're keeping watch on Lord Stephan's chamber," she said.

Cecily's mouth twisted.

Lightning stabbed, brilliantly, several hills away.

"Mustn't go too far," said the woman. "The castellan said you might take ill. Getting cold and wet would only make the danger greater."

Cecily wondered how far the woman would enforce the castellan's decrees, but in the garden, she could not call for help. Cecily walked faster again, into a path formed from tangles of dark red roses. The branches grew so profusely that the servant was forced behind her again.

The path led to the square walled in by the white and yellow roses, bright in the gloom.

"If you tire—" said the woman.

"If I am ailing, being tired would make it much worse. I am weary now. I should rest." Cecily plowed toward the bench.

The woman's dismay made Cecily fight to keep her face unmoved, but the woman would be a spy. She sat.

"Perhaps I should not walk back, after so long and wearisome a walk. Perhaps, if you got some help. . . ."

The woman stared dumbly at her, but did not stir. Cecily sat back. It had been worth a try.

A few large drops of water fell, to splat on the ground. The woman tugged at Cecily's sleeve. Then the rain came, not in drops, but a downpour that soaked and chilled Cecily in moments, turned the paths white with spatter, and filled the air until Cecily could see no farther than the nearest rosebush.

She had wanted a way to be rid of the servant. The woman pointed to an alcove within the courtyard. Cecily nodded and waited. When the relieved woman headed off, Cecily gathered up her skirts and ran.

Her dress was already sodden and cold, but she ignored the slap of the cloth against her legs. Even with her head bent, it was hard to make out her footing—but the woman would cling like a burr, once she knew that Cecily wanted to be rid of her. Only if she could vanish within the maze. . . .

She had turned about two corners before the indignant cry came from behind her. The rain thickened, as if it meant to drown out the sound of her footsteps.

The rain slowed to a steady drum, and she was already soaked to the bone, but when Cecily saw the alcove, its door engulfed in yellow roses, she went to it. She only looked to see that the floor was not flooded before she went in. Brushing by the petals and leaves freed them of the water they had held; they dumped it on her. She stood in the center, dripping, and despite how she had run, shivering. Her sodden hair clung to her neck and shoulders, her clothes hung like leaden sheets, and her shoes might never be the same.

Among the other tragedies you face, Cecily thought. She sat on the bench. Outside, raindrops bounced on puddles. Occasional drips reached through the leaves to splatter on her.

Her finger itched. Cecily wondered what happened in court now. The scene seemed to glitter before her: ladies-in-waiting in white, Queen Blanche herself in brocade and jewels as brilliant as the rainbow; the courtiers in their finery; perhaps an ambassador bowing before the queen. She scratched her finger. The Iltrian ambassador, these days. . . and her hand froze.

The Iltrians might want Lord Stephan dead. The king of Iltria never let things stand in the way of his alliances. Cecily stared at the puddles before her. The rain thickened. It drummed on the ground, peppered the puddles, and broke through the rose laves with heavy, cold drops. The Iltrians might even be right. The queen's weakness for flattery had never led her astray before, but Queen Blanche had never injured a lady-in-waiting before.

Cecily let out her breath. As if the Iltrians could easily reach Clearwater. As if knowing the murderers told her how to deal with the poison.

She considered the unicorn. It could purify water and food. She could hope that it would purify air as well.

She huddled, her legs drawing up. She could not set the unicorn loose on the poison unless Philip and Lord Stephan—and the servants—were out of the way. Most of the servants were men, and women among them had children, and even if there were maidens among the maidservants, they had tongues. She did not want the poisoner to know of the unicorn.

The pebble flew through the air and struck Lord Stephan's window.

Water splattered from the bushes on her. Any servant who looked out would see her and find her odd. Cecily glanced over the windows. Nothing moved, not even in Lord Stephan's.

She scowled and looked for another pebble, but when she looked up, she saw hands at the latch. A moment later, Philip looked out. "What are you about, Cecily?"

"Philip." He eyed her; she must look as sodden as the maze's paths, but she went on. "Take Lord Stephan into the next chamber—not the antechamber. The next suite. Make up some excuse, and take any servant with you. Until I bid you come out, stay there."

Philip scowled. Cecily's heart beat harder. He might have the harder part here, persuading the servant. "Tell him—tell him nothing. Claim your uncle is whimsical and may hurt himself unless indulged."

His scowl deepened.

"Philip, you did not go into the garden where I forbade you. Do you think that worked out so ill?"

Phillip leaned on the window frame, and Cecily wondered how much poison he had breathed, but he nodded.

The rain had stopped, and her hair and skirts slowly dried, but the sky was still cloudy, and puddles spread everywhere. Footsteps rushed down a nearby path. Glad that she wore a drab gown, Cecily pulled back. The servant rushed by, splashing through the puddles.

Gathering her skirts, ignoring how her shoes squished, Cecily darted by, giving the servant only a moment to glimpse her. She did not dare run on, for fear the woman would hear the footsteps, but she hurried down the last paths and unlocked the gate. The unicorn frisked through the bushes, sending raindrops flying, and chomped off a rose branch, causing a small shower. As it munched, water dripping, it looked at her brightly.

She reached for the rope. Her fingers were colder than she had realized, and the rain had swollen the knot. It took her minutes to undo it so she could lead the unicorn away.

Cecily turned. A delicate rainbow spread over the thickest gray of the clouds. She let her breath out.

The unicorn sniffed at the doors. Cecily tugged at the rope, trying to get the unicorn up the stairs. It looked mildly at her. She did not have time for this. Philip could not put off the servants forever. Drawing a deep breath, she picked the unicorn up. It started but did not struggle, and she climbed the stairs two at a time. She held her breath at the top, but no servant guarded the door. She shifted the unicorn in her hands to free one hand for the latch.

She still sensed the foulness, and the unicorn thrashed, its head whipping from side to side. Cecily lowered it quickly. The unicorn bolted over the room. She shut the door, not taking an eye from the unicorn, but it paid her no heed. It galloped about, heedless of the rope it trailed, as if its horn had to touch every piece of air, and scrambled over every piece of furniture that could bear its weight. The foulness slowly sank. The air seemed to grow brighter.

Cecily wondered what the servants thought of the sound, and then the door to the antechamber opened. Neither Philip or Lord Stephan would defy her, but the servants had no warning. The unicorn stopped and looked about the room. Thanking God, Cecily snatched it up again. Her heart hammered as she turned to face the door. The unicorn might not react to a man, or a woman not a maiden, as it did to poison.

The door opened. Dear God, let the unicorn not struggle to kill the man!

The castellan looked at the unicorn and seemed mildly displeased. The prayer died in her thoughts.

"Clever, my lady, but how long do you think it will last?"

Cecily stared at him. His foreign mother—"Your mother was an Iltrian," she said, her voice a croak.

The castellan lifted an eyebrow.

Cecily choked.

"Your finger has healed. You are well enough to leave." He drifted into the room, and Cecily pulled back, against the wall. "Your unicorn can purify only what lies before it. Your efforts have only wasted time—yours and mine."

The unicorn's head moved, so that its horn tracked the man. Cecily could not breathe for a minute.

"There is nothing you can do to thwart me."

Nothing *I* can do, thought Cecily. She worked at the knot in the rope about its neck. The unicorn might trip.

He walked toward her. Cecily shrank toward the door. The castellan seemed to notice only her cringing. "You would be wise to appease me, rather than merely play the fool."

The rope came free. Cecily took two strides, to reach the doorway. The castellan scowled. She lowered the unicorn to the floor, stepped back, and slammed the door. No sound came from within, but when the castellan realized—she grabbed a heavy chair, pushed it before the door, and listened with her heart hammering. Still, there was silence within. Then, she was still close to the unicorn. She gathered her skirts and ran down the corridor.

Her footsteps drowned out any hoofbeats, but she did not get far enough to not hear the scream. It echoed for one sharp moment, and silence came after. Cecily stopped. The servants must have heard that scream, but none of them appeared.

She drew a deep breath. May God have mercy on his soul. Having no more need to run, she lowered her skirts. And now— Lord Stephan and Philip.

The unicorn did not struggle as its dark eyes inspected Lord Stephan and Philip. Cecily still held it closely.

Lord Stephan looked at the body and the pool of blood. He shook his head. "Alas. Such a noble servant of the queen. He risked a unicorn in his efforts to aid me, because the queen wished me to well cared for." He looked at Philip and Cecily. "I will write to King David and Queen Blanche, telling them so."

Philip looked at her arm. Cecily glanced down, saw how the unicorn nipped at the cloth, and shifted her arm.

"He's not the one who ordered it," she said.

Lord Stephan spread his hands. "The Iltrians—are ambassadors. Even if she had proof, the queen can not punish them."

Cecily stroked the unicorn's head. It gave her an excuse to not look up.

"My lady," said Lord Stephan, "your unicorn purifies poison?"

Cecily nodded.

Lord Stephan held out his hand. "Too much of a risk for my nephew, but I must get to the queen."

The unicorn's body quivered with tension. Its horn lowered toward his hand.

"My lord, the danger is being run through. If the unicorn cures you—it is safe for Philip, too."

Her voice trembled. But Lord Stephan might need his secretary.

At times, Lord Stephan's visit seemed like a dream. Cecily stopped among rose bushes much lower than they had been. She had brought the unicorn back to the forest, but signs of its attentions were everywhere.

Her shoes chaffed a little. They had suffered from the drenching.

She sighed. The rumor had even reached Clearwater: in surprise and rage, the Iltrian ambassador treated Lord Stephan so rudely that Queen Blanche dismissed the embassy. But it felt like a dream.

Rose petals floated by her on the breeze. It was late in the year. Soon the labyrinth would be a maze of dry branches.

She still might wander it, then. Keeping the waiting from driving her mad—

She heard horses arriving, but the Queen, on her deathbed, would not have sent for one Lady Cecily. She wandered on.

Voices sounded in the maze: young men and women, speaking in the tones of court. Cecily stopped. One sounded familiar.

Philip stepped from between two rosebushes before her. She blinked, and he smiled. "Have you heard the news, my lady?"

Cecily shook her head.

"It was sent at once to King David, since it most concerns him: the Queen's Grace has died."

Cecily hesitated. "May God have mercy on her soul."

Philip nodded, grave for a moment, but went on. "My uncle sent word to the King's Grace of the Iltrian ambassadors and—other things." He stepped closer; he did not look entirely pleased. "The King's Grace wishes you to return to your post as a lady-in-waiting. Though not to the queen. To the princess. More suitable for a young woman."

"And better company!" Emerging from the rosebushes, a red-haired man smiled at her. "The young men of court do not like the queen's company; they prefer company their own age."

"I met young men as the queen's lady-in-waiting," said Cecily.

Philip's smile deepened. "I think that if the young men do not know you are not lightly wooed, you will be able to instruct them quickly." He took her hand and kissed it.

Author's Note

The dragon in "The Dragon's Cottage" is based not on the dragons out of western European folklore, but those found in eastern European fairy tales. Where they tended to be not the behemoths you find in modern fantasy, but rather closer to human size.

Which has a number of consequences. . . .

The Dragon's Cottage

She sat by the fire. It did not make her feel warmer—she pulled her shawl closer—but the flames, pale as candlelight, shed the only light. At times, she was glad that this was only a low cottage, with four rooms. It was smaller than those of many peasants, but a castle would only hold so many more dark corners.

The low sibilant voice echoed from the doorway. "The horse takes three days, to go, to come, and Midsummer's Day—"

Margarita surged to her feet. She felt colder than before, but if he rode off for Midsummer's Day—"I won't have it."

Silence echoed after her words. She looked toward his voice. Firelight glinted from black scales, from ivory claws—from his eyes. He studied her, though he could doubtless see nothing but a shadow. She swallowed. No doubt he had muttered without thought of her—he did so, so often.

She stepped to the other side of the hearth, so he could see her face by the firelight. "You are a married m—dragon now. I won't have it. You can not gad about after maidens at Midsummer, as you did before you married me."

The dragon edged closer to the fire, became a creature rather than a suggestion made by glints of firelight. The slantwise light carved out deep shadows, and though, on his hind legs, he stood only a head taller than she, he loomed.

"I won't wed this one. I'll eat her."

"Men always say that," said Margarita. After a moment, she added, "I dare say dragons say it as readily."

"I ate all the rest."

"You didn't eat me. You married me."

The dragon reached the fireplace. Scaled and muscled, his ivory teeth and claws bitterly sharp, he studied her. The firelight must make her face as much shadow as light. But he said that his carrying her off had made her his wife.

"I should—" His breath hissed in and out like a boiling kettle. "Your beauty should not have persuaded me—I should have eaten you like the rest."

I wish you had, thought Margarita, and it was bitter in her mouth, but she said, "Should or should not, you did. You are married now." She did not so much as twitch before his gaze. Her father the emperor would not spare this year's maiden, any more than he had spared her. Only she could stop it.

Maybe.

But the dragon—she had demanded nothing, even asked for nothing since he fetched her here. She had surprise on her side.

Dark clouds hung over the fields. Before the wind, grass bent low, toward the ground. Only the pole where the maiden was bound stood upright. The wind blew steadily, from the east where the dragon rode from, but no thunder sounded, no raindrops fell, and no man saw any sign of the dragon, though Midsummer's Day had nearly ended.

"She will starve there," said Theodore.

From the ignominious shelter of the lodge, unlit for fear of drawing the dragon's eye, he looked at the knights about him. "The dragon will not come. Lady Olympia will starve—"

"Sir Theodore!" The Emperor Maximilian's voice broke a path through the courtiers. "Are you, too, meddling in affairs of state?"

Even in the dimly lit lodge, the emperor's purple robes were vivid when everyone else dressed drably, against the dust of the road. Theodore bowed, from duty, and to hide his face.

"Your father should have taken more care. He lost two sons for their foolish attempt to thwart this tragic but necessary sacrifice." The emperor stepped closer. "Your brothers brought about nothing but their own inglorious deaths. Her sacrifice buys us life."

"Her death now will buy nothing," said Theodore. "The dragon will not take a corpse as this year's maiden."

After a long minute, the emperor gave orders: food for the Lady Olympia, and drink. Even that the guards might unbind her at night to sleep.

The emperor went on, "But until the dragon comes to claim her, she will await him every day at that stake."

Theodore was glad the duty was not his. She must have been numb with horror, she had been so pale and quiet on the way here, but to be freed and bound to the post again. . . .

The emperor glanced about the lodge. He came here only once a year, to fulfill his bargain with the dragon, and the place had never been made a fitting imperial abode. "We will leave such servants, and enough, to carry out that task—"

"She will need clothing for winter," said Theodore. "Frozen, she will be as dead."

The emperor lifted an eyebrow. "Clothing, as well." But as the courtiers and servants moved about him, he cocked his finger at Theodore.

Theodore approached, bowed again.

"Your father does not deserve my reproach. He sent you to your brothers' beheadings, he sent you here to witness my own daughter's fate. . . do you wish to leave him without sons?"

What need did his father have of sons? thought Theodore. To keep his noble line alive? But what need did the emperor have for nobility? He would rather sacrifice gently born ladies than let his nobles fight for him.

"It is no shame, being your father's heir; your brothers forfeited their due by their own folly."

"I will meddle no more in this." Theodore gestured at the stake. "I will ensure it. I will leave your lands, and seek out adventures to distract me."

The emperor sniffed. "If you can possibly have enough."

The inn's fireplace glowed a low, dull red, but a single candle shone on the card table. A handful of travelers, shadows in the gloom, gossiped by the fire, but the candlelight shone on the faces at the table and glinted from each man's pile of coin.

Theodore finished shuffling. His own pile had reached twice the size of the next largest. "My last hand."

Groans resounded. "You have to give us a chance—"

"And if dawn comes, what then?" He had never before been so glad that he never played for high stakes.

"Which way do you go, in the morning?" said one man, small and sharp-featured.

"East," said Theodore.

Blank silence followed. Theodore dealt out the cards and picked up his own.

"But," said a hulking merchant's man, "the emperor said that—"

"The emperor," said Theodore, "wants me to get my fill of adventure. The lands the dragon comes from and goes to— nothing could be better suited to giving me my full."

They picked up their cards but eyed him as often as their hands. Perhaps they wanted to ask if he had promised to let the dragon be. He looked at his own cards. He had only said the his leaving meant that he would not interfere with offering Lady Olympia.

He won the hand. Even his usual luck was not needed against such distracted opponents.

Trees towered like a castle's pillars. Far overhead, their leaves blocked the light until nothing, not even moss, grew beneath, though their trunks were so damp as be black.

Nothing stirred, but Theodore's horse shied. He mastered it and looked about.

Under one tree, a woman stood. Her hair spilled like a mantle as black as night. He thought that her gown was indigo, but he could not be certain, it was so dark. Her face was as pale as the moon, and only more vivid by contrast.

She looked at him. With her pale face, her dark eyes made another contrast. He could not read them.

Her mouth smiled. "Only a bold knight ventures into this forest."

He patted his horse's neck. "You flatter me, my lady."

She spread her white hands. "So gallant a knight should not lose his life over a mischance in the dark. There is no inn, but I can offer my hospitality."

She gestured to one side. A cottage sat there, its windows dark beside its low door. It sat in the shadow; he might have not seen it when the woman had drawn his eye; he could not swear that it had appeared when she spoke.

The air did not twitch. No courteous knight would refuse so gentle an offer—and only a witch would live in this forest. Who knew what enchantments she could weave if thwarted?

A shed stood behind the cottage. Once his horse cropped hay in it, he went inside.

Only a fireplace lit the cottage. The witch-woman bent over a stew pot. He smelled venison and mushrooms. In the forest, he had not seen so much as the hoof print of a deer, but he said nothing. She smiled.

"Do you amuse the ladies at court, when you stay the evening?" she said.

"Sometimes we talk," said Theodore. "Or we play cards."

"Cards," she breathed out. The word sounded like a breeze through trees. "Men do not bring cards this far to the west." Theodore reached into his pocket. At the sight of the deck, the witch-woman stilled. "I played cards once."

He bowed. A simple courtesy from a guest to his hostess. "As my lady wishes: to play, or not to play."

Slowly, she said, "To play."

He started to shuffle, and she gestured to the trestle table. He sat on a bench there, and thought, still shuffling, Low stakes. Then he thought, No stakes at all.

The witch-woman sat opposite him, the firelight casting itself from behind, to shadow her entirely against it. "It is the custom," she said, "for the loser of the game to pay a forfeit to the winner."

Theodore started. "Of a certainty not, my lady! How could I demand a forfeit from so gracious a hostess?"

"It is the custom." She leaned her chin against her cupped hand. "We will forfeit—knowledge. The knowledge that the winner wishes for." And she watched him with avid eyes. He could think of one knowledge of him, that he wished quite strongly she would not gain.

He shuffled the cards again. His seat was lit none too well, but he could not ask for a candle. In his hand, he read the cards by shape rather than by color. When he glanced upward, the witch-woman watched him so intently that he wondered if she saw his cards reflected in his own eyes. Never once did he see her glance at her own cards.

She did know how to play, but his skill was greater, and his luck did not fail him. Finally, she threw down the cards and rose to fill bowls with stew. She started to eat hers, but when he ate, she watched him, brooding over the bowl with a spoon neglected in her hand. He ate with his head ducked low.

"Ask me a question, sir knight, and I will answer it."

The firelight, slanting on her face, made one eye glitter and sketched out her pale cheekbone. Shadow hid the other half of her face past sight.

Theodore lay down his spoon. "There is a dragon," he said. He took up the cards. "Every year, he demanded a maiden from the empire. Last year he did not eat but carried off Emperor Maximilian's daughter, the Princess Margarita. This year he did not claim the maiden offered him." He shuffled the cards. Even that sounded loud in the cottage; the fire scarcely crackled. "How can I find this dragon?"

"Ride on the road that brought you this far, sir knight," said the witch-woman. "Past the inn. You will find his cottage." She leaned forward. "Let us play again."

He handed over the cards. She shuffled them herself.

Her gaze was even more intent than the last game. Once he thought he glanced away from a heart and looked back to find it a club, and another time, a spade seemed to turn to a diamond. But the second made his playing easier, and again, he won.

"Another question," said the woman, frostily.

"How can I leave that dragon's cottage safely, after I reach it?"

She twitched. For a moment, the firelight glinted from her other eye, and then he could see it no more. "The road goes past the cottage. It leads to a copper bridge over a dark river, and then to a silver bridge, and then to a gold bridge. Cross the golden bridge, which the dragon can not cross. If he is angry enough to try, the bridge will break under him."

Theodore looked at her a minute longer. He could barely see her in the gloom; he could not read her face.

She shifted. "And you must ride the dragon's horse to reach the bridge before him, if he chases you." She shuffled the cards, once, and held them out to him. Her tone took on a sweetened edge. "And may these cards show their owner what it means to lose."

Theodore watched her a moment. Her extended hand did not waver. After a moment, he realized what an insult it was, to make her wait; he reached out, quickly, to take them.

"And now, another game."

Her voice did not change in tone. He rose, pushing back the bench. "I regret having brought the game to you, since I have displeased you."

Her face twitched.

"Nor, since you dislike my small triumphs, can I insist on the hospitality you have so generously offered."

She started to protest, but he made his way to the door, and from there to his horse. Bad to ride all night, worse in these woods, but he did not dare camp where the witch lived.

The table sat before the fireplace. In the shadows outside, people talked and drank ale, and a minstrel played a low tune, but the card players had their faces well-lit. Theodore could see them all.

When he looked at them. Now, he scowled and studied the cards in his hand. Telling red from black did not do much to improve his play. He could suggest using a different pack, but he did not know what they would think of that.

When, for the third hand, his luck failed him, and a carter hauled in his coins, he was glad for the low stakes, but the smart was sharper than ever he had thought.

"I'll trust, good men, that you have won all my ill luck from me," he said. They urged him to stay—but they had already claimed all his winnings from the first inn. His only good luck was that *they* wanted only his coin.

Hills rumpled the ground about the road. He could see little but the nearest hill. Beneath the thick clouds, dingy yellow grasses bent and straightened at the whims of the winds, and the day grew darker with evening.

There were no trees. He had seen no trees since that dawn when he left the witch's forest.

He rode on. The road wound beside a tall hill, too steep to climb, and veered out, as the hill did—but in that hollow, a house sat.

Theodore pulled up his horse. The cottage was almost the hue of the grasses and little larger than the witch's. He remembered the dragon, coming riding from the east, and eyed the door; the dragon could fit in that door. And there was a stable out back, for the horse. He drew in a deep breath.

The door opened, softly, silently. For a moment, his heart seemed to stop. He had found the cottage, and now he had to face the dragon. . . .

A woman's ragged voice came out, "You do not want to stop here. Sleep beneath the stars, or in the rain. All the rain will do is leave you wet and cold—"

"Margarita?" It slipped his lips before he could control them. He could recognize the voice, he thought, despite the hoarseness of it.

The woman fell silent. Theodore did, as well; that insolence would have gotten his head cut off at court. "Your Highness," he said. "Princess Margarita."

A choked sound came out of the cottage. "Theodore. . . Sir Theodore. Go now, while he is still gone, my husband—"

"Your *husband*?"

She emerged then: Margarita in a gown of pale yellow, her face colorless with terror and showing tears, her golden hair thick about her, as lovely as ever it had been in court. She stood mutely. The wind made her skirt billow and tugged at her hair.

She wiped her hand over her eyes. "My husband. Or so he insists, having carried me off. . . ."

His tongue felt numb.

"Is this so much worse," said Margarita, bitterly, "than the common lot of princesses in their marriages?"

Theodore drew in his breath, and let it out again. "Yes."

She turned away, as if to hide her face. He could not imagine how he could rescue her, but he could not leave her here.

"Your father sent me out of the empire, for adventures," said Theodore. "What choice do I have but to obey him?"

"Guests?" shrieked the dragon, like a boiling kettle. "Guests?"

"No, not *guests*," said Margarita.

Theodore crouched, hidden behind the chest, and his heart hammered. The dragon was an enormous, distorted shadow on the way, but Margarita's shadow was distorted as well.

"Not *guests*," repeated the dragon.

"Well, since it's not *guests*," said Margarita, "it's all right then—"

Theodore closed his eyes. He could see the tender, imploring look to her face. She did not spare herself to rescue him.

"Yes, yes," said the dragon, "as long as it's not *guests*, it's all right, I give you my word."

"I am glad," said Theodore, rising.

For a long minute, the dragon, a shadowed bulk, did not move. Then its tail shifted. Scales rasped over the floor.

"I am not *guests*," said Theodore. "Only a *guest*."

When the dragon did not speak, he said, "I hope I may amuse you. Do you play cards?"

After a long minute, the dragon said, "I have never heard of these cards. How could they—amuse?"

The witch might have done him good, thought Theodore. "Let us play cards together, and I will show you." He looked about, and saw a table. He gestured at it. Long moments later, marking by the beating of Theodore's heart, the dragon walked over and sat on a stool there.

The fire lay even lower in this cottage than it had in the witch-woman's. The dragon was a shadow as they played; when he shifted, light picked out now a black and scaly arm, now ivory-colored claws, now an eye intent on the cards, but easily able to be as intent on him, or on Margarita.

Silent, she sat by the fire, her hands folded in her lap. Theodore said nothing more than was needed for the game. As the dragon won, and won, and won, he added to his words happy little hums and hisses of pleasure. He shifted more often, and Theodore pondered being crushed under him.

After the seventh game, the dragon sat back. The firelight lay over him and picked out his gleaming shape. "A fine game."

Theodore shuffled the cards again. He had saved himself for a time, but neither he nor Margarita could escape.

He shuffled the cards one more time, and was ready to deal. The dragon watched him.

He sat up. "It is a custom that when playing the game, the loser forfeit something to the winner. I did not mention it before, because it does not befit one who knows how to play to insist on it with a novice. But, clearly, you have mastered the cards. The loser can forfeit."

The dragon's mouth twitched. Theodore could not see the shape clearly enough to know whether it was a smile, but he could see the teeth.

"I can think of no more fitting a forfeit—" He bowed his head and held out the deck.

In the silence, the fire crackled. Theodore wondered how it dared.

Delicate_y—a mother could not be more delicate with her newborn—:he dragon reached out. Its ivory claws took hold of the deck and drew it back.

Theodore wondered how he managed to breathe, but he did. Then, he even managed to suggest another game to the new owner of the deck.

"It is—improper," said Theodore, "for the forfeit to be of less value from one than from the other. Yours to me should be as unusual and valuable as mine to you."

The dragon coiled into himself, looking more like a metal statue than any living thing, except for his gleaming, bitter, eyes. Its breath came in and out, harshly, hissing.

"Her," the dragon said, abruptly. "Take her. My wife."

Margarita twitched, but Theodore did not dare look at her. He laughed, low. "How many kings are there? How many have daughters, and beautiful daughters? No, the only thing at this cottage that is as unusual as my cards is your horse."

This silence lasted longer. His own heart, as bold as the fire, drummed ir. his ears; he wondered that the dragon did not hear it.

The dragon's breath hissed out again. "So be it."

Margarita rose. "I will fetch more wood for the fire, that you may play."

Theodore rose and bowed to the dragon. "While she fetches it, I will see my new horse, as you saw your new deck of cards."

He had to take care, in the shadows, even as he walked to the door. The dragon lurked behind him, brooding, glancing now and again at its deck of cards.

In the hallway, Margarita breathed, "You would rather have the horse than me."

"He said he would give me you," whispered Theodore. "He did not say he would not take you back again. With the horse—he will not reclaim it—or you."

In the hall, only the faintest firelight reached, but it touched Margarita's face long enough for him to see her smile. Hand in hand, they stole down the corridor to the stables.

"Stand by the door," he whispered, and went for his tack. The dragon's horse swiveled an ear, but it must have known his claim; it let him saddle and bridle it. He heard a rumbling sound, like a pot rising to boil, but he took his own horse to the door and freed it, so that it would not starve, and the dragon would not ride it.

The noise grew louder.

Theodore mounted the dragon's horse.

A bellow of outrage burst from the cottage.

Theodore clapped his heels to the horse's sides, snatched Margarita up, and rode down the road, toward the bridges.

Hours later, it did not surprise him, much, when the golden bridge shattered, and the fall of its shards hid the falling dragon, but could not drown out its cry of rage.

Dragonfire and Time

The cave gleamed ferociously. All about, gold and silver, rubies, emeralds, amethysts, and sapphires shone. The center of it all, the dragon shifted like quicksilver; every fiery scale on her body glinted with motion. Even her black eyes, like liquid, shone as she looked at the only drabness in the cave.

The wizard, in his sigil-marked brown robes, held out his staff as if that would fend her off. The dragon breathed orange fire, too bright to look at, and the wizard charred before Mae's gaze.

The vision cut off.

Mae gasped for breath. One day, she would *murder* Gregor for showing her these things; she hated, hated, *hated* them. He could just *tell* her.

She looked about. White-washed walls, windows letting in sunlight and not a gem in sight except in Gregor's hand—she let out her breath. She and Gregor had sigils on their clothes, but on prudently short smocks, not robes. The room, with its tables and shelves, looked like that of a tidy clerk—if you did not look out the windows at the wheeling birds.

Gregor studied the gem in his hand. "The dragon is displeased."

The king was bound to deliver justice to the dragons. That had been the bargain that kept them from ravaging the countryside with fire and slaughter whenever a thief offended. Still—

"She seems to have dealt with her problem," Mae said dryly. "What does she need to be appeased?"

"The wizard," said Gregor, "survived." He put down the gem with a click.

Mae blinked. Only a very powerful wizard could survive dragonfire. Then, survive was all that he had done; the dragon had burned him; she had seen that clearly enough, and shuddered.

"Not even return spells could restore those burns. What penalty does she want?"

"This happened twenty-odd years ago," said Gregor, "at which time she was content with that as punishment."

Mae cocked an eyebrow. Gregor looked back at the gem.

"Since then, she has seen him. Recently. She says if we do not deal with the thief, she will come after him."

Mae sat back. Six generations ago, a dragon had come after a robber; it was still a byword. And King Carolus's most famous deed was persuading the dragons to abide by his justice. . . .

Which meant, since the king could not chase after every thief, the king's men had to wreak that justice for him. Particularly his wizards.

Gregor touched the stone. "She enchanted a gem out of her own hoard to send to us."

Mae flinched. A dragon willing to do that was angry beyond belief. Still, she needed to know more.

"I know that dragons have sharp eyes for thieves, but how can she know that this one is her culprit?"

"She saw him look as he had before the fire. Also, she *smelled* him."

A dragon could not be mistaken there. Mae let her breath out. "I don't suppose that any of him was left behind—charred or what have you. For a similarity spell."

"She didn't speak of it. And it would be in her lair if there were."

Mae scowled. Gregor should send a wizard more powerful than she was. The thief had saved himself from dragonfire. Dealing with him called for a master wizard, not a young one, new in the royal service; she was still working off the years she had spent in the royal academy for wizards. And spells for hunting down strangers had never been her strength.

Light glinted from the gem. If Gregor were willing to send someone else, he would have summoned someone else. She was not so new to the royal service as to not know that. Softly, she let her breath out. He had not even said that wizards more fit for the task were too busy for it.

"The dragon must say *where* she smelled this culprit," she said.

"By the Bay of Stars," said Gregor. "The dragon lairs in the mountain, and she saw him in the city. Recently."

"Within a month or two? He could be anywhere by now."

"I have confidence in your abilities," he said, his bright tone making his actual indifference clear. "You'll be in time for the spring festivals—they hold them late, there. And Imogene is stationed in the city. If nothing else has happened, you can call on her for aid."

"Better," said Mae, "that's where Christopher lives. And that's where the cave and its crystals are."

Gregor scowled. "His ability to scry is—limited."

Mae lifted her eyebrows. "Isn't that why he's there? Because the cave of time improves scrying?"

"He's there," said Gregor, "because a wizard has to watch over the cave of time. It does us no good at all to contain the harm that magic does to time if we let it *grow* there. In time, it would destroy all."

Mae folded her arms. She had learned this the first year in her studies. Which meant that she knew that "in time" meant in centuries. And any wizard could have protected it. Sending one who could scry was not to protect the cave.

"He must scry something else, besides," said Gregor.

"Sometime more urgent? A fire-breathing dragon could distract even Christopher."

"Then you must deal with the dragon before it bothers him. If you take the night train, you will be in time for the spring festival's beginning."

Mae stood and sighed. As if that would be a benefit. The festival would be a time of abundant magic, making it all the harder to find their thief in the uproar. But she calculated what she would need to pack. Things for spellcraft, a knife for when wizardry would not suffice, and if she could work out what spells she might use—

"First, his face from the stone," Mae said. "To show Imogene and Christopher. We might do a similarity spell."

"Hope springs eternal, does it not?" said Gregor.

I thought, Mae thought, that you had confidence in my abilities.

He went on. "Also, you must stop on the way and assure the dragon that we will catch her thief."

Mae scowled. "When will she strike?"

"She didn't say. We must catch him as soon as possible." Gregor's mouth moved into something intended to be a smile.

Mae looked woodenly at him. No one who considered her skills would send her as a diplomat, least of all to appease a dragon. At least, no one who cared.

She nodded, left the room, and walked to the elevator.

A woman, one she vaguely knew, already waited there. "New assignment? The dragon?"

The elevator chimed, and they stepped inside.

"The dragon," said Mae.

"No wonder. You have mastered ward spells better than anyone else in the king's service."

"I learned about dragons, too. Cast a ward spell where a dragon can see me? Let one know that I want to be protected from it? I might as well rob the lair from the start."

The other woman raised her eyebrows, the elevator stopped at the ground, and she headed off. Mae watched her go. Angelica, she though:, her name was Angelica—but Angelica would not help her.

In the valley, grass and wildflowers still grew, as high as her waist to either side, the grass lushly green, and the yellow and white flowers nodding in the wind.

Mae straightened her blue smock, with its golden sigils that would afford her little protection, but would not alert the dragon. Then she started to climb. The road was steep and rocky; she kept her gaze on her footing, without glancing ahead. Steadily plugging onward brought her to where the grass was withered and dry. She set her shoulders and climbed on. That formed a narrow band. Beyond, the stone had been burnt black.

Unlike their thief, she wore breeches, and her smock was not long; she wondered that the thief had climbed this.

Perhaps he had not. He had reversed dragonfire, which argued some power. His robes might not hinder him.

She closed her eyes a moment. She wished she could check the stone, but she remembered mud on the robe hem. Perhaps not powerful in all forms of wizardry.

"Ho! Lady!"

Mae blinked. From the valley, a weather-beaten shepherd waved and called again. "Leave, lady! There's a dragon up there!"

"So there is," said a deep and sibilant voice behind Mae. The shepherd blanched, even beneath his deep tan, and hurried his flock off.

Mae let her breath out. Her back itched, but she only managed to turn slowly.

The dragon coiled over dark stone. Cloudy though the day was, the stray sunlight glinted from every scale, awaking color that would shame the opal. The stone's vision had given Mae no notion how large the dragon was. Seeing her loom over the wizard, in a tiny crystal, was one thing; to have her loom over herself, her scales scraping on the stone, was another.

The dragon's breath puffed at her, hot, inquisitive little breezes.

Mae bowed. "I have come to tell you that we received your crystal, and now we hunt your thief for the king's justice."

The dragon breathed, in, out. "My crystal."

It felt like a coal under Mae's smock. "Unless you wish to reclaim it, and put off the day of his capture, we will use it in catching the thief, and return it with the word of him."

The dragon's tongue, long and black, and as thin as a sword blade with a forked end, licked the air. "Soon."

"How soon do you wish us—"

The dragon's head lunged forward, within inches of her face. "SOON."

"If," said Mae, "the sooner is the better, perhaps we could cast a return spell in your lair, and summon him back."

The dragon jerked away.

Perhaps indeed. They would need something of him to use in the spell, and then a far more powerful wizard than she was would need to cast the spell.

She fought down a smile. Then, the dragon would never consent. "If not, I must use more leisurely methods."

She waited the length of three heartbeats. The dragon's tongue licked the air again, but she did not speak. Mae bowed again and walked down the hill.

She did not run.

Though she felt the dragon's gaze on her back every step of the way, she did not run.

Only at the bottom, with grass closing about her, did she sigh. She had not gotten a time from the dragon. She might be followed in a year, a month, a week, or even a day.

The train station lay ahead, through the hills, and she trudged toward it.

Once, she would have listened to the tale of this with rapture: a brave young wizard meeting a glorious dragon, and then hunting down a wizard and thief. She had dreamed of becoming such a wizard. Her mouth twitched. Dreams left, but duty remained.

Mae stared out the window.

Dawn light, a gray turning ever paler, glinted from the bay; the day would be fair, of course. Perhaps even so without spellcraft. The windows half-reflected the people who passed her, overlaying the lake waters. A clump of girls, giggling, ran forward in finery as colorful as flowers, and whispered that she saw the city, no she did not, yes that was it, you could even see the garlands. . . .

The ruddy shades of the city, thought Mae, were almost certainly brick.

The train clattered on. And on. She sat back before their excitement infected her. She had seen many festivities in her day, and visiting one while on the king's business meant it would serve only as a pother to make her work more difficult. Her clothes would betray her place if nothing else did; she had dressed for practicality.

The train pulled into the station, where a crowd waited beneath its vast clock. Brilliant flowers and banners bedecked the buildings about, and men and women draped still more banners, or strung garlands. Passengers surged from the train, to merry greetings, with much kissing and embracing, and crowning the newcomers with flowers, and then the crowd surged back into the city street, bearing the newcomers away.

Near the end of the flood, Mae walked into the morning sunshine. The air, still chilly, smelled of blossoms. The buildings about were brick in every shade of red, and laden with flowers.

How much more beautiful it would look if only she were not here on the king's business. Her bag felt heavier than when she had started.

The dragon would burn that crowd as easily as it had the thief, she reminded herself, dutifully.

She heard a loud snort. Imogene, her pale brown hair streaked with gray, wearing the drab blue robes of a royal wizard at work, walked over. "I didn't quite believe that Gregor would send another wizard."

"Of course not," said Mae. "You're a wizard—you can handle wizardry."

"So cynical, so young," said Imogene.

"I notice you don't say—so inaccurate."

Imogene shrugged before glancing up at the clock, and then across the city, to the city hall. Mae frowned. They showed the same time.

Imogene's mouth quirked into a half-smile. "Didn't they warn you? Of course not. Never trust a clock here without comparing it to another. Not just in the city, but outside, too. For leagues."

As they started into the city, Mae glanced back, checking the doorways. The railroad station showed a few uncommon wards. One used runes of time. "The cave of time?"

"Oh, yeah. Not often, but too often for ease. A mayor once asked us to move it—"

Mae felt her face contort in surprise. "The cave was here first. It's why the city's here!"

"The city is no longer here only to hold inns for wizards who want to scry here," said Imogene dryly. "*Your* wizard, for instance. He hasn't tried to consult Christopher."

A crowd of young men crossed the street ahead of them; dressed in black, wearing crowns of pink flowers, they passed a jug from one man to the next. As black as soot, thought Mae.

"A pity you can't count on him revealing himself in the festival," said Imogene. "Or even coming out of whatever hole he hides in."

Mae reflected on the image in the stone, before the dragonfire, and spoke slowly. "He might—come out at least. He made himself young again, and hale—and handsome. He wouldn't have spent that much magic to hide in the shadows." Three little girls chased each other, giggling, across their path. "Revealing himself, that I grant you. Easy to lose yourself in these crowds, even if you were far more marvelous than he is."

A fiddler and a laughing cascade of dancers blocked the way ahead. Imogene darted into an alley. Mae followed, into the narrow and dank way, but glanced back at the swirling skirts and ribbons.

"You and I should have dressed more festively."

"What a way to hinder work," said Imogene, stepping wide to cross a puddle.

"The better to hide in the crowds," said Mae. She picked her way over the cobblestones.

"In due course—but Christopher sent for you. We can stop by the cave on the way."

Mae gave her a sidelong glance, but the buildings shadowed Imogene's face, making it unreadable.

"Gregor told me not to do that," said Mae, though she plugged on beside her.

"Gregor didn't know what was happening here."

Mae shrugged. "I'll come. I hope I'm not interfering with anything you should be doing."

Imogene snorted. "Gregor sent me here to use my judgment. And Christopher was already getting nowhere, slowly, about simulacra."

Simulacra, thought Mae. That, at least, had nothing to do with her task.

A crowd billowed around the corner. A breathless young woman, trailing flowers, crossed Mae's path, not too quickly that a young man could not follow her.

Said Imogene in her ear, "Why did Gregor send you *now*?"

Mae thought of repeating what Gregor had said about the festivities. As if it had not been a fudged up excuse. She shrugged, shifted her bag between her hands, and looked about instead.

After some time darting about crowds, or billowing banners, they turned a corner. In front of them, no building stood, though everywhere else they were built wall to wall. Here, trees and greenery grew. A handful of white blossoms, ragged but sweet-smelling, sprouted on bushes, and no one had dared pluck even one for the festival.

Imogene plunged within, the leaves rustling about her, and Mae followed. The narrow path had branches poking out from either side. When they passed some stones, Mae glanced down. Runes. She wished she could learn what wards surrounded the cave. She might never face another time when she might use them, but still, they were runes of protection.

She looked back to the path. Next to it, a stand of asters bloomed purple beneath a tree turning scarlet. Not perhaps as good wards as could be laid, though no one would let a wizard as young as she was try to improve them.

Imogene had gotten ahead while she maundered. Mae hurried, reaching her at the ivy-covered cave mouth, where the stone was black. In the green-tinted light inside, they descended into the shadowy cave. The stone paled, from black to dark gray, and then still lighter.

Light flared ahead, a pure white. Mae's breath hissed between her teeth.

Moments later, Imogene called, "Morning, Christopher. The train—for once—arrived on time."

Mae followed her into the cave. The center was vaguely round, but dips and hollows extended from it, and on the stone, crystals gleamed. Most were dots like stars. Others grew as large as her thumb; in them, white fire flickered and flared.

Christopher turned. Still the same mild man she had met when she first entered the king's service, though his hair and beard held more white in their iron than then. He nodded to them. Behind him glowed yet another crystal. This one was as large as her fist—no, larger than both her fists. White lightning crackled inside it.

"That one must be strong," said Imogene uneasily.

True, thought Mae. The cave trapped the flaw when magic twisted time awry, but capture did not suffice; the only cure was to bring the cause in touch with its crystal. She had not heard about the clocks, but the teachers had included the crystals in their lessons.

"It is strong, but also, it is near. Perhaps even in the city." Christopher sighed. "I have yet to find it."

Mae's stomach curdled. The king did not keep a wizard here with no other task but to tend the cave because the magic was minor. And to deal with this, they would not have picked any wizard who came to hand.

"I would take it kindly if you watch while you wander. If anything seems out of place in your labors today, consider this as well as your thief-wizard." He looked at Mae. "Also, this cave helps with scrying, and I heard you had the face of the man you seek."

"The dragon sent a crystal with it." Mae laid aside her bag, and undid the belt on her smock and the buttons on her vest. "A crystal from her hoard." She pulled out the pouch. "And when I spoke with her, she did not like it, but she let me keep it to aid in the search."

Christopher stared at her, not on the bag. "A dragon was angry enough to send *her own gem*, and Gregor wants me to look for blood simulacra?"

"Blood simulacra?" Mae felt like a parrot.

Christopher blinked. "You make simulacra by similarity—and the best way to make it similar to someone is by blood."

Mae nodded, pondering. Similarity was strongest when it was not similarity but identity, except that—"Using identity to create similarity has *interesting* effects on spells."

"I don't know what the effect is on this spell, but someone must have figured it out. The spell's unlawful. Gregor found some wizards cast it anyway, and terminate the simulacra before they last seven years."

Mae flinched.

Christopher went on. "He wants me to learn—"

"All that pother," grumbled Imogene. The light cast sharp shadows across her face, carving out heights and depths. "Over a law that no one knows why it was passed, and I'm caught up in fighting it too."

Christopher shifted, facing her, and was silhouetted against the light. "If we don't know why the law was passed, we can not possibly know that the reason was bad."

"Fools pass foolish laws." Imogene shrugged.

"In which case," said Christopher, "you should consider whether folly is hereditary."

Imogene opened her mouth again.

"The dragon," said Mae, "will burn simulacra as easily as it does everything else—whether they've lasted seven years, seven months, seven days—seven minutes!" She stepped forward. Her shadow loomed and whirled on the cave walls. "And we don't have long. The dragon wants him caught—'soon.'"

Imogene gave her a foul look, but Christopher nodded.

"I will scry." He gestured at a nook, and Mae saw that the shadows there half-concealed a passage. "I can always call it practice to help with the other work."

They started to climb up the same rough stone they had climbed down to reach the cave, and the way darkened as they walked.

Christopher's voice echoed. "Still studying your ward spells, Mae?"

"Some I've mastered," said Mae. "Still prophesying wizards' futures by their spells?"

Christopher chuckled. "Imogene, get her to work while she's here, and get all the wards you might ever need from her." He climbed a sharper slope. "Wizards who favor ward spells—they marry young, have large families, and leave the royal service to cast wards."

"I've yet to leave," said Mae. "You said that years ago."

"And Gregor concentrates on scrying," said Imogene. "Which must make a wizard live alone. Me, I find it much more useful to learn what would be useful."

Christopher opened a door. Behind, the stone had been carved into rooms. Furniture, and gloom, filled them. In a side chamber, he lit a lamp. The golden lamplight touched a table and half a dozen crystals, which did not glow.

"Scrying ones," he said. "They never *were* in the cave."

Mae nodded. "Those vanish if they are resolved."

Christopher smiled. "I see they still tell the new wizards *some* things."

Mae's smile felt forced. Old Dora had lavishly described how a beautiful young woman had turned to ash, not even a bone left, when a crystal from the cave had been brought near her.

But Christopher already bent over the scrying stone, and it showed tiny figures on a tiny street. She hurried over to peer with him. Scads of tiny figures—she had thought the crowds large when they came here, but now revelers packed the flower-laden streets. And Christopher shifted the vision, seeking. Mae did not dare blink, and the twists and turns had her clutch the table against dizziness.

"We'll stare at this until we have cricks in our necks," said Imogene.

"If you prefer sore feet—" said Mae. And then—"There! Who's that?"

Christopher shifted the scene back. Young men and women—with a flower crown, she would pass unmarked in their number—crowded a square with splashing fountains. There, the wizard stood, surrounded by laughing young women. Beneath a crown of wild roses, he looked less merry than they were, but more handsome than in the dragon's gem, handsome enough to explain their attention—but the gem had shown him years ago.

She pointed him out to the others. From their faces, she did not have to explain the ages.

"It appears our rogue studied after his failure," said Imogene. "A powerful return spell, to keep him young."

"A powerful return spell," said Mae, "to undo the dragonfire. After that, peeling off twenty years must be easy."

Then, she had difficulty turning flowers back to buds. She might be glad that her ward spells were good. "Maybe he's taken advantage of the cave. It's a spell based on time."

Christopher paled.

The crowd laughed. The conjuror lay dry branches on the stage.

Imogene eyed the packed square. "The quickest way around is—" She scowled in thought.

Throwing the petals over the branches, the conjuror intoned words, and flowers formed. Mae's breath hissed through her teeth. Not as buds swelling and blooming. As wilted petals rejoining and forming flowers again—a return spell, she thought. The petals primed the branches for the spell.

The conjuror broke off twigs to throw them to the crowd, who called out in wonder and jubilation and snatched the flowers from the air. For a moment, Mae remembered how marvelous that would have seemed, when she was small.

"Wax in your ears?" said Imogene, tugging on her arm.

Mae scurried after her, down the side street. "No, just watching the terrible waste of a return spell. He conjured real flowers—"

"Something to throw to the crowd," said Imogene.

"He could throw illusions," said Mae. "Everyone will be too drunk to remember how long they lasted."

"Ah well," said Imogene. "Gregor will remember *our* spells."

Mae's mouth twisted. Once upon a time, she would have stopped to admire the beauty of the flowers, the mastery of the wizard. Now—she just thought she had no need to master that skill just yet.

On an ordinary day, the fountains, cascading water on white stone, would have filled the air with sound. This day, the air held too many other sounds—squeals, chatter, and even music floating in. Garlands of flowers trailed over the steps in. Some shed petals as Mae and Imogene walked down.

The crowd of the young had grown larger since they had seen in the stone; one man played a lute, but no one tried to dance, not in this crowd. Mae surveyed the faces. The wizard still stood there. She was as certain as the dragon had been.

She drew in her breath. She had not thought that the wizard could look quite so young, or so innocent.

Then, his appearance at the festivities showed his vanity.

"Look at how the girls gawk," said Imogene.

Well, thought Mae, he was handsome.

"Tam, you can't leave now!" called a woman. Their wizard shook his head and stepped away. Others implored him, saying that he couldn't go, that they had barely met him.

Another woman held out her hands. "Promise us that you will come for the dancing."

Mae could not hear what he said, but she could hear the laughter in his tone. Women laughed; some men looked jealous. Tam pulled away and climbed stairs on the opposite side of the square.

"Looks like—" Imogene grabbed Mae's wrist and muttered an incantation; she was gone, except for her grip, and Mae could not see the wrist she held either. She glanced quickly about. A couple of revelers blinked before turning back to the festivities.

"Remember that you are audible," said Imogene, "and worse, tangible."

Mae heard Imogene's footsteps and followed. Now and again, an invisible foot crushed an already wilting flower, but soon, Tam picked his way through tiny side streets, all less crowded, many deserted and lacking decorations. Fewer people to confuse with the spell, thought Mae, as she hurried to catch the corner where Tam had turned—past a heap of broken leaves, someone had made a garland there, or tossed aside the waste—and he went down yet another street.

Cricks in their necks *and* sore feet, thought Mae. Gregor could have found a wizard better suited to this task. She hurried on, after him, through the labyrinthine streets, across bustling squares, under falls of flower petals.

Then, in a wall-lined street where tree branches reached over the walls from gardens, Tam let himself into a brick house. Mae let her breath out. In one garden, a dove cooed.

From the air, Imogene said, "We must memorize that house."

"What?" said Mae, playfully; "no chalk marks?"

"Even on common doors, they would be noticed," said Imogene, as solemn as a judge. "A wizard would take them as sigils. As for magic marks—"

Mae looked at the house again. The bricks on this street varied from one building to the next. This one had bricks the shade of a pale red wine. No trees grew high enough for her to see branches over its walls; she was not certain it had a garden. Carefully, she paced out the street, to mark the distance. When she reached the house, she smelled something green—a garden then, and one with pungent herbs, but the wall held no door, not even one of solid wood.

Whatever the wizard grew in there, he did not want anyone to steal. She could not recognize the smells, which was a pity. Some herbs would forewarn her of his spellcraft. She sniffed the air again.

"If you're *quite* done," said Imogene.

In the cave, Mae leaned over the table again. She was getting the crick in her neck. And it would be worse before they were done, she knew.

"Even this is dangerous," said Christopher. Still, he let the crystal show the house. The bricks' pale red looked distinctive enough.

"Can we see the garden?" said Mae.

Christopher shifted his hands and frowned. "No."

After a shocked moment, her heart started to pound. A powerful ward indeed, to prevent scrying of a place open to the air. She would never venture such a ward; she had never attempt to learn one. She did not think there were more than a dozen wizards who would, and only in dire need.

She wondered how much this Tam knew of the cave, and how it affected magic.

Christopher lowered his hands. "That tells you something there. And—there's magic about the place. Some of it is rather nasty, but lawful—wards—healing—"

"Healing?" said Imogene and Mae at once.

"Perhaps," said Mae, "the spell doesn't last. He has to keep casting it. Or at least renewing it." She straightened. Her neck creaked, and she cocked her head, stretching it. "He left as if a spell were about to end."

She thought, for a moment, of telling the dragon that the spell came and went, that the thief still suffered *some* of the time. Then her mouth twisted. She would need a ward as strong as the one on the garden—stronger. She looked at the others.

Imogene sighed. "Well, we must trap him." She spoke to Christopher. "He looks a flirt, and he's about Mae's age. She could get near him."

Mae thought a moment, and nodded. "And I'm the strongest at wards."

Imogene blinked, as if she had expected an argument.

"First, we make a tracking spell so that whatever happens, you can still find me." Her fingers rubbed together. Against this wizard, she wanted them to able to find her wherever she went. "A drop of blood would do the trick."

"Not here," said Imogene. "To keep the cave from interfering with such spells is exactly why the royal post is not on top of the cave."

More walking. Already. "Then," said Mae, "I can cart my bag while we go to ready the spell."

In the royal post, a vast room held crucibles and alembics, and jars with a miscellany of magically useful things from dried rose petals to imported spices. Herbs hung from the rafters; smelling more of dust than pungency, they must have come from the summer before.

Imogene pothered about, fetching this and that and stirring up dust. Mae looked out the window. From the outside, the post was, if a bit large, still a white-washed and half-timbered house, even bedecked with flowers like any other; she must look like any maiden, gazing at the festivities. A fresh garland hung over a withered and trampled one. Mae's eyes narrowed. After a moment, she leaned out the window, her wand in hand.

"What are you doing, Mae?" said Imogene.

"A test," said Mae. She chanted the return spell. The withered garland shivered, took on fresh, new shades of green and pink, and shuddered as petals and leaves took on new life and lifted up into the air. A scent as delicate as a seashell reached her, but she frowned. The spell had flowed far more easily than any return spell she had ever cast before.

She pulled back in. "Testing a return spell. That conjuror was not so foolish, to have cast one. The cave must affect them."

"I could have told you that," said Imogene.

"Why didn't you then? Knowing that might tell us how he overcame the dragonfire."

"He overcame her *somehow*," said Imogene, gloomily. She scowled at her handiwork.

Mae looked back at the garland. Lovely and sweet—she sighed. When she had been a child, she had gawked with wide eyes at any such spell. One that did it so well would have left her dumbstruck.

She sighed.

Revelers traipsed down the street, their arms linked, and those caught before them had to run aside or be caught. A man at the end waved a jug at Mae. "Eat, drink, and make merry—"

Mae smiled, wryly. If she did not catch her thief, they might not put off dying until tomorrow. She drew back by the door. A shadowed window reflected a pale shadow of her, and Mae grimaced. She did not need a clear reflection. She wore a gray gown—better than her working clothing—but even with the pink crown of flowers, she did not look a flirt.

The line lurched by, and Mae stole from the shadows. Young women swirled down the street. One threw a hand in the air. Flowers foamed from it to the street. The others followed, and the street filled with conjurations, half-formed, ill-formed, brightly colored but plain. Whether they had scent no nose could tell, with the floral scents on every breeze.

"Join the fun," said a maid, waving at Mae's wand.

She had to look as if she had come to celebrate, Mae reminded herself. Nothing that would distract her too much. She waved her wand. Gold and silver sparkled and scattered; the spell was easy to cast, commonly known, and briefly spectacular. The women exclaimed. Mae loaded the air with the lights and sidled by, toward the fountains, where the dancing would be.

The sparkles faded, and Mae looked about. She wished they had had time to cast another spell, so that Christopher could speak to her.

"You're a wizard," said a voice behind her.

Mae hoped that she did not start too badly. At least the voice—a young man, she thought—had not drawn any other gazes, and merriment continued, noisily, all about them. She turned, trying to look idly curious.

Tam studied her. He looked as intent as when he had faced down the dragon in its lair, but he had not looked so worried then.

She could feel the color seeping from her face. Her hands clutched at air as she fought against snatching her wand and casting a spell—any spell that might protect her.

She forced out a laugh. "That little thing? Bright but simple, any conjuror could cast it." She glanced through her lashes at him. If she lured him somewhere where he would think that he could strike, then she would see what he would do. "I could teach you it—"

And then we will see how powerful my wards are, she thought. Her heart hammered. She could not tell whether it was excitement or terror. She wanted to allure him—she reached for his hand.

He did not put his hand out. He did not draw it back. He only shook his head.

Mae let her breath in and out. He had come to her, not she to him; he had some purpose; she should learn it and hope it betrayed him. A cascade of sky blue petals, filling the air with sweet scents, tumbled from a building and blew past them, their hair and clothes snagging this one and that. Tam did not seem even to notice it.

"You didn't cast it like a street conjuror, I can't—"

Had the dragonfire addled his wits? Mae uneasily wondered whether that would appease the dragon, or if she would have to deal with a man too simple to fathom his crime. She reached out with more decision. Her hand caught his, and he did not resist. She drew him out of the way. Nothing adorned this alleyway, shadowed by the buildings and chilled by the shadows; puddles formed on the flagstones, and stray leaves and branches lay beneath windows, discarded as unneeded for garlands and crowns.

Perhaps their retreat looked like romance to the on-lookers; no one commented on them that she heard, and no one pursued.

Her heart still hammered.

"It was—you cleaned up your spell," said Tam. "You didn't leave scraps of it about like a street conjuror."

"I just made my spells tidy," said Mae. "You do not want to look a fool."

"No conjuror cares whether he looks like a fool before wizards," said Tam, "and only a wizard would tell."

A moment passed; her heart beat once, twice, thrice.

"A wizard, or me," he said, sounding miserable. "But I do not expect you to believe that."

Mae said each word with care: "Who are you?"

He met her gaze. "I wanted to ask you that."

After another heartbeat, Mae said, "I am—"

Tam shook his head, fiercely. "No. Who am I?"

It was as if the clamor outside had shifted to another city, far away. Nothing made sense, and Mae could not steady her breathing. Tam looked more bewildered than she had ever seen any man or woman. A breeze skittered by their feet, carrying petals like scraps of sunrise.

This could be a trap, she reminded herself. Never mind how innocent he looks, or how charming he is. And if it is, he's as crafty as a fox.

Tam was still silent, and waiting. Mae forced her breath out. She had not gone hunting for him in order to keep herself as safe as possible, and her hand still lingered on his.

She pulled him through the shadows, into an empty square. Milky petals cascaded from aging garlands, or lay brown and crushed on the stone, from feet that had left.

There she turned again. Tam seemed still bewildered, but no more than before—as if her actions seemed sensible to him.

"Who are you?" she whispered. "First, where do you come from?"

"I live in a house in this city," he said. He described it, and in one thing, at least, she knew he told the truth.

"Alone?" she said.

"No."

Mae stiffened.

Tam looked as if hunting for words. "With a—man, I think. He wears heavy robes, and a cowl—I've barely seen his face, and never by daylight." He drew a deep breath. "He was furious when I got a glimpse. He has terrible scars—"

"From burns?"

Tam started, and she had spoken too loudly. If she could prove this to the dragon—but Tam did not know the need. She swallowed and gentled her voice.

"Could you tell?"

Tam shook his head. He looked so lost that she had to remind herself that he could be lying, could still *be* their wizard and thief.

"I am afraid to ask. I think he is a wizard." He met her gaze. "My first memories are of that house, but something is wrong. I think something has been wrong for years, but I have just noticed—"

Witched, Mae thought. Before he wailed, she said, "How long have you lived there?"

He let his breath out. "Seven years, I think."

Mae brooded. After the theft. She eyed him again. He looked like their thief. And if not—she had just talked with other wizards about simulacra. Many a wizard could make something that resembled a man, and could look innocent, winning, and pitiful, but that no man should pity because it felt no pain.

She let a ragged breath out. Imogene would say that his handsome face distracted her, but she could not ignore Tam in hopes that he was a simulacrum and felt neither pain nor joy. She glanced at his face. A simulacrum suffered no pangs of conscience, either.

"How old were you when you first were there?" she said.

"I do not think I have aged a day since—" He looked imploringly at her.

He's not—Mae did not complete that thought. If this were a cunning plan, it was cunning enough; it would trap her. She considered. She needed a secluded place, to hide any secrets, and to ensure that revelers would not haul them off to separate festivities.

"Follow me," she whispered, and stole over the cobblestones. Not the royal hall; she might as well shout her plans from the main square. She hopped over a heaped garland that would make footing slippery. And she could not bring him anywhere truly secret, when he might still be a thief.

Imogene appeared in their path, and her wand was in hand. Tam stepped backward.

The lowness of her voice did not make it gentle. "What do you think you are doing?"

"Learning what our thief is up to," said Mae. Tam blinked, and Mae pointed at him. "I think he can tell us, but we do not want him to do so in the open."

Imogene's eyes narrowed, and her mouth opened.

Mae said, "He would consent to having his wizardry bound."

Tam blinked.

"He doesn't look ready to consent," said Imogene, dryly.

"Would it help you?" said Tam. When Mae nodded, "Then, yes, of course—what will it do?"

"Keep you from casting spells," said Mae, even more dryly than Imogene.

Tam started to laugh. And laugh. Eying him, Imogene took his arm. After a minute, she told him to shush. He choked and gasped for breath. Imogene slowly released his arm, watching him every moment.

"I thought—the octagon," said Mae. As casually as if she had often brought things there, over years, she thought. She fished in her pocket.

"That's as good a place as any," said Imogene.

Mae pulled a piece of string out. Always useful, was string. "Your hand," she said.

Imogene said, "You thought of binding his wizardry only when I found you?"

"What wizardry?" said Tam, holding out his hand.

Mae looped the string about his wrist and concentrated on the spell; it was a ward, and among the first she had mastered. She should have thought of it. *Knowing* the best wards in the world did her no good.

She looked up. Tam studied his hand and the string. Imogene watched them like a maiden aunt about to scold.

Mae almost wished she had kissed him. No doubt, onlookers would think they were lovers. She looked down, and hoped the faint heat in her cheeks was not too visible.

The building appeared ahead of her, ready for the king's wizards. It did not show the magical uses to which it could be put; even the octagon was an interior room, not visible through the ivy-covered walls. Mae, her heart pattering, picked out the door and unlocked it. She stepped within and held the door open.

Tam walked through it, into the white-washed hallway, lit by a handful of windows. He looked about as if he had never seen anything like it before. Not even, as she had, other buildings built specially to contain wizardry.

Imogene stepped inside, glancing at Mae as she passed her.

Mae closed the door and locked it. She spoke even as she slid the key away. "He told me, before, that there's a man who lives in that house. He's—" She gestured at Tam. "—seen something of him, enough to tell that he's badly scarred. Perhaps burned."

Imogene's breath hissed out.

Tam looked between them and down at the string.

"Who was he?" said Mae. "Why does he have you with him?"

"His name is Thomas—and why? To act for him," said Tam, promptly. His words slowed. "To be for him—so he could live through my eyes—" He let out his breath. "He babbled. A lot. As if he had been alone a lot."

"You would have been wiser to listen!" roared a rough voice. Mae whirled about. To live through Tam's eyes—she should have guessed that the silencing would not affect him, any more than it did Tam. She would have had a moment to prepare, and have realized that he would attack here, before the strong protections would seal him out.

The wizard—Thomas—loomed in the corridor, against the white walls. He still wore brown robes, but a tattered and filthy one, as if he did not care. His hood shadowed his face.

"Wiser to ask *me* than to sneak about." Thomas raised his staff, his gaze intent on Tam. Mae snatched her wand. "But still a fool to have questions at all! Your place—"

Imogene shouted a spell. With one hand, Mae tossed up a ward; with the other, she hauled Tam back. Even if he knew any wards, she had bound his wizardry and left him helpless. She breathed hard, glad that at least Tam had come meekly. If he had resisted, and Thomas had struck him down outside her ward—

Imogene's hands glowed with silver-green fire. Mae gasped. She had not realized that Imogene could cast such a spell. She inched backward, urging Tam with her. The blaze would, mostly likely, not overwhelm her ward, but best to give Imogene a free shot.

Thomas pointed his staff, and spells flooded from his mouth like a river's water over a waterfall. Imogene's fire lashed out, but Thomas thrust it aside. It gushed against the wall, sparkling brighter than the day. Imogene cast a ward spell of her own. Mae trusted that it would not interfere with Imogene's magic. She did not know that fire spell well enough to know that her ward would not.

For that matter, she had no ready spell to cast. A brawl, one they *had* to win, and she did not know how to fight

Thomas's hands emerged from his sleeves. Burnt, bony, showing the breath of dragonfire. She would never have known him for their thief by his face. She glanced at Tam. How similar—

A pure white light flared. She could not look; Imogene faltered and stepped back, and when the light failed, the walls were singed. Imogene looked unharmed but pale. This Thomas had mastered many spells. Imogene readied another spell of fire—of magical fire, not quite so brilliant as dragonfire.

Mae blinked. She glanced from Tam to Thomas and back. Whatever else Thomas had done, whatever other spells he had mastered, he had made a perfect similarity between himself and this Tam, whoever, whatever he was. Her hand tightened on his arm as she reached for a pin. They were right when they said she needed that, and pieces of white cloth, as much as string.

"I need some blood," she said, her voice low, "to deal with him."

He looked at her, his face bleak, but did not resist. "Whatever you need."

"It will hurt."

Tam mutely held out his hand. When she pricked him and caught the drops on a white cloth, he said, "It's not too bad."

"That's not what will hurt," said Mae. She drew a deep breath, chanted a return spell, and threw the cloth into Imogene's enchanted fires. She held her breath. Magical fire at least—though she had no dragonfire, she hoped this would serve, that it was close enough for a return spell, this near to the cave.

For a second, it fluttered like any piece of cloth, but it reached far enough, and started to burn. Smoke looped up. Imogene grunted in surprise; Tam cried out, sharply, and gasped, but she managed not to look aside to him; Thomas instantly started to smoke and, in moments, started to burn in orange flame. The air smelled like roast meat, and he screamed in agony. The noise echoed so loudly that Mae barely kept her wits about her, but she drew her knife, ducked under Thomas's flailing arms, ignoring the heat, and stabbed.

His scream was choked off. Blood spilled from the wound. Mae remembered her lessons, held the knife tightly, and drew back. With the blade no longer holding it back, blood gushed, and Thomas started to fall. She gasped for the cooler air. Her face felt roasted.

Hands grabbed her from behind, getting her away. The blood still splashed, but Thomas fell face-down in it, without bearing her to the floor. Smoke curled from the corpse.

Imogene snatched the cloth out of the air and quenched the fire. The smoke stopped.

Mae breathed in—the air, however much cooler, was foul with ash—and out. "May God have mercy on his soul." Her voice was flat.

Tam's hands loosened.

"Thank you," said Mae, and he looked away. She studied his pale face and then looked him over with care. If the similarity had been close enough, the return spell, and another enchanted fire, might have burnt Tam as well. But she saw no smoke or charring.

She looked back at his face. A moment later, she put a hand to his arm and yanked him toward the door. With her free hand, she unlocked and pulled open the door, to shove him outside, just in time. Tam fell to his knees, shaken by nausea, and was violently ill under the vines.

"Wretched youngsters!" called a querulous voice across the street. An old man shook his staff at them. "Taking any excuse for your drunkenness—"

Mae gave him such a baneful look that he tottered off in silence. Tam, still pale, straightened. He did not rise.

"Was—was the pain that bad?" said Mae. She could have killed him. Dangerous as letting Thomas go free would have been, it would have been her hand that killed Tam.

Tam shook his head. "I don't feel it anymore. It was—" He looked back through the door, at the body, and shuddered.

He *had* lived in Thomas's house, but Mae still looked uneasily at him.

"Who are you?" said Imogene to Tam. "*What* are you?"

Tam flinched.

"There are many things he can not be, such as a simulacrum," said Mae. She pointed. "He's dead." Her hand swept back. "He's still alive."

Imogene nodded. "Some spells would have ended with him," she said meditatively.

Tam looked at the floor. Mae felt sick. She could have killed him twice over. And now—duty called her.

"For now," said Mae, "Tam is our way to show to the dragon that she has no grounds for offense."

"A dragon?" said Tam.

"Thomas tried to rob a dragon," said Mae. "His scars are dragonfire. You resemble him before the dragon burned him." She leaned forward. "The dragon saw you. And was angered by the sight."

Tam flinched. He understood that, at least.

"If we take the night train, we can get there by morning." She looked at the body. "Bring them both, I think. No doubt they *smell* the same."

Before dawn, gray mists curled about. Even the green valley looked dreary. Then, she was exhausted. Mae looked up the mountain and thought both coffin and Tam would be hidden from where she had met the dragon, even if the mists cleared.

"Stay here," she said. Tam nodded; he looked as gray and weary as she felt. Mae started to climb, with mists curling about her. They thickened until she could see no sign of either Tam or the coffin, and still she climbed up, and up. Past where the dragon had found her, and still up. Black earth surrounded her;

she did not think she could have seen the valley's green even
without the mists. In the air, pink touched the grayness. Mae
stopped, wondering how far she had climbed. Did this path even
lead to the lair?

"Oh dragon," she called. Her voice echoed, further than she
might have expected. "Oh dragon."

Her heart beat, loud when nothing else stirred. She *had* not
arrived too late; the dragon would have started burning with the
valley below.

"Oh human," said the dragon, her voice sardonic.

Mae turned. The gray about the dragon only made her seem
more brilliant by contrast. Mae bowed and pulled out the bag
with the gem.

The dragon stiffened. "Do—" She leaned forward, sniffing.
"Do you claim to have—found—my thief?"

"I have two things to show you," said Mae. "If you will listen
what I tell you of them, you will be satisfied."

The dragon lifted her head. "I smell—"

"I will bring it here," said Mae. "If you will allow me time to
tell you." She did not budge. The dragon's eyes narrowed. "The
king will not uphold an unreasonable claim."

The dragon's voice rumbled. "If you do not satisfy me—"

The dragon's head swiveled. Tam stood without flinching,
though his face was pale, and he never looked up. The dragon
eyed him from every angle. Her tongue licked the air, as if tasting
his smell, or that from the open coffin.

"They smell the same," said the dragon, petulantly.

"But they are two," said Mae. "And the one who is dead is
your thief. We could not have burned him like that. Not with
our spells."

The dragon eyed it again.

They could not duplicate dragonfire, and the dragon would not admit it if they could, but the more often the dragon asked, the more miserable Tam looked, and the more Mae wondered. Some kind of magic, but he looked and acted like a man—

"This coffin does not adorn your mountain," said Mae. "I will fetch it to a graveyard."

For one long moment, the dragon did not twitch. Then her breath, hot and metallic, gusted out. Mae's hair flew, and Tam, directly in the blast, staggered.

"Go," said the dragon.

Mae stood by the train, letting it empty entirely before she even tried to get into the other car. The railroad workers glanced at her, and away, without speaking at her. The noon sun shone on the square, where the last flowers wilted. No one waited on the platform to go on, for the other way. Though she had no doubt that if the platform were crowded to await a royal progress, they would still have ensured that she would get that off their train before she left.

While they shifted the coffin, Tam said, "What will you do with it?"

"A burial," said Mae. "Even a burial service. One can always hope that he repented."

"Will I have to look at him again?"

"No." They started to trundle it down the street. Mae was glad the festivities were gone. Even with wizardry, getting it through a crowd would have strained her.

Imogene appeared out of a cross street, striding toward them. "Did you *know* what he had in his garden?"

"No door," said Mae. "I tried to smell it—but *someone* hurried me along."

Imogene sliced her hand through the air. "One could wish that your dragon felt suitably grateful for our hard work. Some herbs deserve only to be burnt with the hottest fire available."

She eyed Tam. "And Christopher wants to see *him*."

As they walked through the greenery to the cave, Imogene's mouth pursed. Mae did not blame her. To bring Tam, still unknown, to a place as magical as the cave of time—

Tam stared at the asters, and the now leafless tree. Imogene said, sharply, "We're expected," and plunged through, to the cave.

The vines stirred. Christopher gestured them just inside, and there they stood. Awkward, perhaps, for four, but Tam was not deep in the cave.

Christopher studied him for a long minute, without a greeting. "Like a simulacrum."

"Simulacra," said Tam, "end with the life of their master." He hooked his hands on his belt.

"A blood simulacrum does not," said Christopher. "That much I have learned." His gaze was steady on Tam, steady enough to unnerve Mae. "When similarity is, in truth, identity—"

"I'm not Thomas," said Tam. "Thomas knew things that I wanted to know—if I were him, I would have known them."

"Like gets like. The same get—the same," said Mae. "Like a child, after its kind—" Her breath hissed out; she added up years and likenesses. "Tam. You were troubled by what Thomas was doing, when you noticed it, recently."

Tam nodded. His head hung.

"You lived there seven years," said Mae, "and nowhere else before." She turned to the others. "He's seven years old." Tam blinked, the others gawked, and Mae added, "He did not notice because he was under the age of reason." She managed a smile at

Tam. "You can hardly be blamed for what you did not notice as a baby."

"I'm not a baby," said Tam.

You don't look like one, thought Mae. She was certain enough that her stomach did a lurch.

"If you are but seven years old," said Christopher, "you are a child. It would explain why they would kill them—"

Tam flinched.

"It would explain something else. Come." Christopher started down. Tam followed him. The women looked at each other for a moment before they followed.

The light came sooner, lighting up their way almost all the way to the entrance. When they descended, the glow filled the cave. Mae held up her hand to shield her eyes. The already large crystal had grown.

"Tam—go and touch that," said Christopher.

Tam walked across the cave; his footsteps echoed, and the light was not so brilliant that Mae could not see his shadow. The footsteps stopped, and light dimmed. Mae swallowed. After a minute, she lowered her arm. This would teach her to flirt when she was about the king's business.

A boy of six or seven looked at Christopher. The crystal in his hands cast shadows across his face. Mae's breath hissed between her teeth. Tam's becoming his true age had not ended the flaw in time.

Christopher knelt before Tam, frowning. "It still thinks something is wrong," he whispered; even so soft, it echoed. "You are too young to go alone—" He picked the boy up and took a few steps, hard to see in the brilliance. And then the light slowly vanished, and they were gone, as if neither one had stood there.

Moments inched by in the sudden gloom.

"*What*," said Imogene, "are we going to tell Gregor?"

Said Mae, "Nothing that will make him happy."

The train slid by the lake's shore. The waves rippled under the sunset, colorful as flowers on one side, dark as night on the other. The crowds were as eager as they had been last year, many rising to look for their first glimpse of the city. Mae, slumped in her seat, was no more happy to be there.

Perhaps less. Gregor had not been pleased; a happy dragon did not offset Christopher's disappearance. And if Gregor did not care that Tam had vanished—she did.

The train came into the station. Once again, she was the last person off it. She slung her bag over her shoulder. She had to find Imogene and tell her that she had come, nominally to see that all was well, and then to enjoy the festivities from the beginning.

She trekked through the streets and felt weary. The garlands awaited the dawn's fresh flowers, but banners were already hanging; the evening turned them black, and they billowed ominously in every breeze, fluttering overhead. She hurried toward the royal post.

"Mae!" Imogene stood in the doorway. "I didn't realize that the news had reached you."

"News?" said Mae.

Imogene blinked. The breeze gushed by her, and she shrugged. "Probably quickest to show you. Come."

Mae stashed her bag and found Imogene already heading down the street. She followed, and Imogene led her toward the cave of time.

"If it wasn't for the news," said Imogene, "what did bring you? Not another dragon?"

"I told Gregor I needed to see that all was well here." The trees appeared ahead. "Has it been hard, this last year? I know Gregor did not send help."

"Hard?" Imogene snorted and pushed through the greenery. "Hard doesn't cover it—but Christopher's back." With a flourish, she pulled back the vines. Mae blinked, knowing that Gregor could not have received *that* news, but stepped forward briskly.

They descended. The glow did not reach them soon; the cave itself was illuminated, but more dimly than any time in her last visit.

Christopher, standing in the middle of it, looked over. "Mae! Imogene did not say she was expecting you."

"She wasn't," said Mae. "I did not know—" She studied him. A year would not account for the white in his hair, or the lines in his face. "What happened to you?"

"The crystal bore me off to fix a flaw," said Christopher. "It did not find that it had made another one, doing so, and so I could not return."

"What flaw?" said Mae. "It had already turned Tam into the boy he really was."

"It thought him a man now. He had to be a boy—some years back. It carried us back those years."

Mae blinked.

"I did some things over the years," said Christopher. "More things than I had years, which is why I did not return soon after I left." He smiled. "I brought my godson."

"Godson?" said Mae. "You have changed."

"It's ready," called a voice down the other stairs. Footsteps followed. Tam stopped on the steps and studied Mae. For a minute, he looked puzzled, like a year ago. Then he smiled, and not a shadow of his old bafflement remained. "Mae."

Christopher laughed. "Be flattered, Mae. He did not remember Imogene by name. He barely recalled her face."

"He remembered you," said Mae.

Christopher swept out his hands. "I have spent the last fourteen years a second time. I hunted down blood simulacra and used crystals to turn them into children again. Because I found them near their births, I did not find myself endlessly going back in time. I arranged foster parents for them and visited them—especially my favorite, my godson, the one who showed the most promise as a wizard."

Tam grinned.

"You kept your work from Gregor," said Mae, her voice thin. "He knew something about the blood simulacra was being kept from him. That was why he set you to scry it."

Christopher chuckled. "If I had told him, how would he have sent you? And if you had not come—it was you who discovered the truth. But now—it would not harm time, and reason would say that Tam is Thomas's rightful heir. Especially since that means a wizard can deal with the wizardry that Thomas left. Imogene and I have settled matters, about the house."

"And," said Tam, cheerfully, "I wanted to see what I could remember."

"Do you remember the festivities?" said Mae. "The dancing?"

"No," said Tam. "But you can show me."

Her tongue touched her lips. "You will disappoint the ladies, not remembering them. They were discontented last year, that you left."

"They already know I do not remember them, they have seen me in the street." His smile deepened. "They have said I must come to the dancing—but I should bring you as well, since you had so little chance last year."

She felt a smile slowly forming on her face. "No chance at all—I would be pleased to join the dances this year."

The Sword Breaks

Eh, don't worry that much. You never know. Happened to me, you know. Did me no harm.

No harm at all, you doubting young pups.

Was after I fought the wyvern at Greenbridge Wood. The fight was hard enough, I was new to knighthood, but it didn't wound me. . . and then it was dead.

Well, I stood over the corpse of that wyvern, with wings and scales and tail flopping all over the ground—blood dark all over my sword, and puddles of it on the ground—and me bone-weary from the fight—and she popped out of nowhere, right before me in the woods. Looked like she couldn't rightly make up her mind whether she was a moonbeam or a maiden. Face looked kind of human, but like a mask, too—didn't look sad, didn't look angry, didn't look happy, didn't look like nothing but a mask. Didn't look down at the wyvern either. Or at my sword. Didn't seem to care, I thought.

So she says, "Your sword will break when you need it most."

Yeah, some knights, old gray-beards, say that the only way a knight keeps from getting cursed is dying young, but this was *me*. Young and immortal, I was. Thought like you were thinking.

Well, one thing never cured a curse—fretting. And life didn't stop since a pup of a knight got cursed by a fairy woman. So I went on to the next thing, and the next after that.

Etins, dragons, trow—saving princesses, saving princes, saving kings and queens—no matter where, no matter what, my sword never broke on me. And if I was laid up with a wound, or wasn't weary enough to sleep as soon as I hit the blankets, I'd wonder, late at night, what it was, that I would need my sword more than

I needed it ever before. Wasn't as if I weren't in danger of my life often enough.

Sure, I thought of switching swords, it wasn't some wizard-made or fairy-blessed blade, but even without that, they're not cheap, and being a knight's not as rich as you think. And once I helped a hedge wizard, and he gave me counsel instead of copper: it might not matter. She hadn't said that sword, the sword I killed the wyvern with, but *my* sword. Could mean any sword I carried.

So then the weather witching came. You've seen it, the places where it blew down all the trees, years ago, and the trees are all saplings still. Every wizard who could was wizarding away against it, and they sent for the wizard of Whitewood. Famous wizard, big on weather, they figured if anyone could do it, he could—and they waited for him, and waited for him, and waited for him.

They figured the *one* way he could be kept out was wizardry.

So they sent this wizard, Diamond, since she wasn't good with the weather, but she could find things. And they sent me with her, since finding things wouldn't keep her safe.

I shoulda figured then, since we needed this wizard like nothing before, but those storms—they drove the curse right out of my head. What with the way you couldn't walk anywhere without leaves flying by 'cause the wind had blown them off the tree, and you were lucky if nothing bigger blew by, and trees falling over on folks and houses and bridges—and anything else you might want to not have a tree fall on.

Diamond's wizarding led us straight to a cave in Whitewood. Out of the wind, all earth, with roots all over the place. And some roots held down the wizard, and some gagged him up. He tried wriggling and talking and stuff, but those roots kept him down.

Which kept me looking about. 'Cause if the same wizard did this, that did the storms, he knew all sorts of wizarding. Dangerous, those ones.

Diamond ran over, and roots jumped up, made a cage 'bout them both. Thick cage, layers of roots—I could see, but I couldn't put my sword through. Couldn't cut 'em either—roots were hard as rock.

Then there was this roar, and a forest drake tried to bite my head off. Looked like this wizard was caught by folks with lots and lots of kinds of wizarding, and willing to use it all to keep him there.

But they got themselves a young forest drake, it would never have fit in the cave otherwise, so I dodged that bite and fought it then, and it was no worse than the wyvern, and I won.

But when it was thrashing its last, it knocked my sword against the cage.

Hard.

And the sword broke.

Cage was fine, wasn't even dented, but my sword—pieces.

I stood there with nothing but the sword hilt, with just a couple inches of blade, in my hand—looking for whatever came after, where I would need my sword the most—

And Diamond said that the roots on the wizard weren't like the cage, she could cut them.

If she had something to cut them with.

Well, I looked at the cage, and all its roots and how they writhed around. You could barely put a hand through. Couldn't put a dagger, or a sword—and I took that sword hilt and slithered it into the cage.

Wasn't easy. Couple of places, I thought I'd gotten in a tangle, even just a couple of inches of blade and a hilt, the roots were that twisted up.

But it got through, being only a broken bit of a sword, and not the whole thing—just when I needed it to do that most. And it cut through those roots like nothing else. And you knew what he did next.

Guess she did mind the wyvern's death—just not the way I'd fancied.

That's why I've got a sword made by the wizard of Whitewood himself—and why you shouldn't care too much when a fairy woman says something.

The White Menagerie

Her dove gray dress faded into the background and ensured no one took her for a lady. She hoped. She had to get through.

Maya sidled along the wall. Courtiers who glanced at her quickly looked back to other courtiers, in white ruffles and ribbons over white silks, satins, and velvets, set with pearls and moonstones. Pale blond hair in ornate coiffures bore white hats with white ribbons or artificial flowers. Ladies hid pink smiles behind fans of white feathers, and glanced over them with gray or watery blue eyes. Mirrors multiplied them and the pale burning candles, the vases filled with dry flowers, silvery in shade, and the silver gilt glittering on the walls.

Laughter and gossip rose. Some, no doubt, arranged marriages or planned taxes. It did not matter to a poor relation who could no more influence them than she could—pick her way through this crowd, it seemed. Maya bit her lip and wished Lord Dariko had said more than that he needed her at the menagerie.

"Why," one languid voice drawled, "there's no need for Lord Dariko to dress his poor relation in gray. Look at her eyes."

Maya flinched and looked at the wall.

"Ah, you can not, she is ashamed of those dark eyes—like a cow's."

"Or a deer's," said another.

The first lady laughed. "A deer? Such a gawky, rawboned woman? A deer is graceful with its dark eyes. Cow eyes—"

Maya picked out a side door and darted into the servants' corridor. Any courtier would die rather than be seen in it, and so it held safety. She forced her breath out and hurried past servants in gray and servants whom the courtiers never saw, in grimy brown.

The courtiers had not gossiped about the menagerie, so the need could not have shamed Lord Dariko, or at least, the knowledge had not escaped. Her teeth worried her lower lip. She had cast enchantments to ensure that all remained peaceful, not even the fluffy white cats troubling the raucous white parrots, but enchantments could be broken. If Lord Dariko had ignored her careful instructions—she knew whom he would blame. With a lecture about the honor of having this menagerie in the royal palace itself.

She came about the corner. Two peacocks, like ghosts, surged onto the roof and their white tails splayed over the tile. Maya hurried inside.

No more raucous than ordinary, with no frightening screams—at least, not frightening to her. Flocks of birds and clutters of cats all about. Little white foxes in a corner. A white wolf, its fangs bared as it snarled; she should check its enchantments. In the very back, Lord Dariko stood next to something chained.

Maya ran.

For a moment, she convinced herself that it was a bear—then that it was a lion. Then she could not fool herself about the gryphon's sharp beak. Its lion body was gigantic, with its shoulder coming as high as her head, and its eagle head towered over her. Its golden eye glared. White feathers, white fur—

"This will do nicely," said Lord Dariko. "Lady Tatyana will not have seen *this* before."

"It's dangerous," said Maya, her voice leaden.

He shrugged. "That's why I sent for you, to enchant it."

"It's still dangerous." She studied the power of its jaw. She should have refused to enchant the wolf. That might have convinced him that her enchantments could not make everything safe. And, unenchanted, the wolf would have been less dangerous than this.

"You know how important Lady Tatyana is," said Lord Dariko. "If her father had not stayed on his estates, like a wild lion lurking in the woods—with his support, the king could have swayed half the nobles to his side. And the things he could have done." He shook his head.

Maya wondered which taxes King Karlon thought he could impose, or which laws he thought he could enforce, with Lady Tatyana's support.

The gryphon glared on, at her, as if it realized Lord Dariko could not subdue it with enchantments.

"We must win this lioness." Lord Dariko shook his head. "God forefend that she throws her influence against—no, if you are obstinate, I shall just lend my own support to King Karlon. He has his treasures, his pageants, his garden with its flowers— she will not have seen the sapphire lilies before or the traitor's rose—"

Maya's hands twitched. A poor relation such as she would never be allowed in that garden, which, perhaps, was just as well. The temptation to raid it like an herb garden—

Lord Dariko's words flowed on. "Nothing can be left to chance. We can not give up the gryphon. I will do my best, whatever you do." He shrugged. "Doubtlessly, you know the value of your enchantments better than I do."

Maya closed her eyes. She heard footsteps and reluctantly opened them again. A servant, his brown clothing splashed with blood, edged forward with a tray of raw meat. The gryphon, with an eagle's cry, lunged forward. The tray clattered on the floor, and new blood showed red on the servant's jerkin. Maya bit her lip. More blood seeped out to stain the jerkin.

"I will enchant the gryphon," she said, tonelessly. For a moment, she toyed with saying that she needed a flower from the royal garden to do it, but that would be a lie. She left lies to the courtiers.

Dariko did not so much as looked pleased at persuading her. Maya wondered if he ever realized how much she restrained her use of enchantments.

The servant bowed to her. She wondered whether he was grateful, or feared Lord Dariko, who insisted that she was his poor relation, not his servant. She straightened. Then if she were a servant, he would have to pay her. She might even save enough to leave.

The gryphon gave an eagle-like cry.

Then, what would he do about the gryphon?

Maya studied the crowds below. No one would noticed her, watching from the window; every courtier and King Karlon himself looked only at the coach.

Lady Tatyana descended from it. She had not traveled dressed like that. Even so grand a lady would not wear a white gown that swept the ground and bore so many furbelows and furs, not while she traveled. Nor keep her pale hair swept up like that, with a hat—Maya thought the things on it were meant for artificial flowers. They used the same fabric, but in twisted shapes no flowers bore.

Then, thought Maya, a great heiress like Tatyana could hardly have her hat adorned with ordinary artificial flowers. Why, some might think she wore plain ordinary *true* flowers.

As dainty as a court poet could wish, with watery blue eyes, Lady Tatyana looked about. Her pallid mouth pursed, suggesting that all before her looked unsatisfactory.

Lords bowed and scrapped. Ladies curtseyed with no thought of the dirt tainting their pale skirts. And when Lady Tatyana made the shallowest of curtsies, King Karlon quickly took her hand to raise her.

Though, thought Maya, the length of her skirt meant that even so shallow a curtsey would get dirt on it.

Courtiers spoke with Lady Tatyana, musicians played, servants offered fine pale wines, and her face did not twitch. She drank a cup of wine, but only when presented with it; she did not ask for more.

Lord Dariko bowed. The plumes on his hat brushed the ground. King Karlon nodded, gesturing toward the door.

Maya gathered her skirts and plunged down the stairs to the menagerie. Peacocks screamed raucously, and she darted within. Cats looked malevolently up from saucers of milk, as if it were her fault they had no meat—as if it were her fault that the kitchens provided no white fish for them—

"As if," she muttered, "the kitchens thought they had enough to do: merely supplying the king and court with the grandest feast in many years! Doubtlessly I could endear myself by going to complain after this...."

The cats stalked off, as if weary of her silliness.

The gryphon glared at her still. The enchantments left it looking stupefied, as if drunk, but had not sweetened its temper. Maya sighed. If this room had a door that led to a courtyard, or even a large window, she would have freed it from chains and enchantments, last night.

"And if," she whispered, "I had a place to go, any refuge at all, I would have ridden you to freedom."

She heard footsteps and stepped nearer the wall. Dariko had taken off many chains; the gryphon only bore one, about its neck, and that one, none too heavy.

"The menagerie," said King Karlon, grandly.

The gryphon shifted, and the chain glittered. Maya gave it a sideways glance. Was that *gilt*?

"A little place of amusements, with some charm." King Karlon's voice carried, and birds sprang up, crying out. Here and there, feathers drifted whitely down.

"Your menagerie," said Lady Tatyana, languidly. Her head turned to survey the room, but slowly, as if the effort exhausted her.

With Dariko hovering to direct them to each beast and bird, they eased through the room. The wolf bared its fangs. Maya wondered whether she had thought too much about the enchantments on the gryphon, leaving her no time to check the others. Still, the wolf did not lunge or snap at the air. Tatyana gave it a cool glance and moved on.

The gryphon received the same cool glance. That rosebud mouth stayed pursed.

"An unusual beast, I suppose," said Lady Tatyana.

After her father's estate, she would be a poor judge of what beasts were common. Maya knew King Karlon would not say that. She kept her face carefully smooth and wondered if the king would even dare *think* that.

"I wonder that you keep such a marvel hidden here." Lady Tatyana eyed the chain. "It could be led about by that, to let the court see the marvel."

For a moment, Maya felt certain that her heart had stopped. Then it thundered in her ears, and she did not care what Lord Dariko thought. She stepped forward and curtseyed. Lord Dariko's eyes narrowed.

Before he could speak, she said, "Your Ladyship. The gryphon is—dangerous."

Lord Dariko chortled. "Such tender care! Forgive my poor orphaned kinswoman, Your Ladyship. The enchantments on it are quite strong, even if not visible to her."

Lady Tatyana's mouth twitched. It could not be called a smile, and not only because nothing else in her face moved.

"Such enchantments as we use to master these beasts—"

Not all of them, thought Maya. Some you try to master with festivities. Some of us you master with the threat of hunger.

"She knows they are safe—but she is fearful." Lord Dariko bowed.

Lady Tatyana inclined her head. "Then, many a servant thinks that danger is a spice, alluring their betters—" Her lips parted. "I will crown her efforts with success. Let us bring the gryphon with us."

She tried to lurk in corners, to keep watch on the gryphon, but courtiers crowded round Lady Tatyana. Her toes sore from being trod on, hiding in the servants' corridors, Maya miserably hoped that if screams started, she could press through the crowd before too much happened.

Their precious Lady Tatyana, who stood the nearest, would fall first. If the gryphon attacked, Maya would not arrive in time to save *her*. Maya wrapped her arms about herself. King Karlon and Lord Dariko should have thought of *that*.

Music sounded, a silvery fanfare from trumpets, and the company cried out in surprise. Maya peeked again.

Something glittered in a servant's hands: a golden sword with a pale sapphire like a fist in its hilt, the enchanted royal sword. After it—more treasures. A golden bird sang; ladies hid their faces behind their fans, before they were caught staring with interest at it. Stones of pale blue and white that glowed on their own—and Maya smirked. The royal treasury had more wondrous stones, shining more brightly, but they were rubies, emeralds, and deep blue sapphires, and such color was unfit for this assembly.

Maya glanced at Lady Tatyana. *She* had no need to hide her face with her fan. It hung by her side, untouched. With the gryphon sitting by her, she toyed with its chain.

The pageantry swept out, and servants began their long rehearsed play. Courtiers, with carefully exaggerated gestures, yawned as if they had seen pageants every night of their lives. Maya sighed. The lion that laid its head in a lady's lap would not seem such a compliment as was intended, not with a tamed, or quiescent, gryphon next to the actual lady.

Then Maia yawned herself.

She leaned against the doorframe. The courtiers had not risen as early as she had, and she had had to work. It was no surprise that she tired before they did.

She stared blankly, seeing nothing. She had laid her best enchantments on the gryphon. She had every reason to think they would hold; her enchantments had never failed. She was being a coward—

Why not, when Lord Dariko had impressed on her the importance of all going well?

Maya yawned again. After a minute, she told herself that an enchantment miscast by a weary enchantress could do as much harm as the gryphon.

Maya cracked her eyes open again, to eye the moonlight and guess how long she had slept this time. But the gray light suffusing the room had to be dawn. She stared at the roof, where the old whitewash looked more brownish than even yellow. The court lay silent; only servants would move about at this hour, and with cat-like stealth. With a groan, she threw her arm over her eyes. She wondered if she had slept straight through an entire hour of the night.

When, after a minute, she had not gone back to sleep, she rose. She could follow the festivities again. Most of them. She doubted they would let her in the garden, but still she could be close enough to hear—

Her hands froze in the act of pulling on her gown. Then she yanked it on, tugged a comb through her hair, and ran from the room.

The royal garden with its marvelous flowers, like the traitor's rose. She could never use the traitor's rose in an enchantment, not if she could pick it as easily as a wayside flower. The rose broke enchantments with its mere presence.

Her enchantment on the gryphon would not last a minute if they took it by the rose.

Maya bit her lip. They might not go to the garden today, but Lord Dariko had been right: the king would show Lady Tatyana the marvels of the garden, sooner or later.

King Karlon had to know of that. They called it the traitor's rose because a traitor had used it on a king. But as she plunged through the corridors, she could not shake the certainty that he would not think of it, or if he did, he would appease Lady Tatyana first.

No courtiers were about, but servants were. Maya seized the closest and questioned them. Yes, of course, the king and his guest went to the garden this day; yes, of course, Lady Tatyana would bring the gryphon.

"Whatever she *says*," said a maid, "she's never parted from it."

"Doesn't King Karlon *know* what the traitor's rose does to enchantments?" said Maya, waspishly, and frightened the maid off. She sighed and continued down the corridors. She had to intercept the king's party before they entered the garden.

If she could not persuade him. . . .

Her hand formed a fist. She had to intercept the king's party before they entered the garden.

A man came out of a room ahead of her—a man in dove gray, one of Lord Dariko's clerks. He bowed. "Mistress Maya, you must not linger here. You were underfoot last night; nobles spoke on how you hung about. You must not be a nuisance to your betters again—"

Maya turned and strode off. Quickly. Before she ended in a
dungeon. Her hands clenched until her nails bit into her palms.
Nothing could help now. She would not be close enough to
subdue the gryphon—and she could do nothing for those in the
garden. The traitor's rose would keep her from casting
enchantments as surely as it would break those on the gryphon.

Light glinted ahead, from swords. Maya blinked. It had taken
that to break into her thoughts? Uneasily she eyed the door. An
ordinary room, she had gone into it more than once, but now
half a dozen guards stood with swords ready, glaring because she
had started down this corridor.

Then she remembered the royal treasures—the bird, the
sword, the gems—paraded before Lady Tatyana last night, and
laughed. The guards shifted uneasily. King Karlon would not
want those safe in the treasury. It would take hours to fetch one
out again if Lady Tatyana expressed the faintest interest. Better
to keep them here and terrify the guards to keep the room safe.
They looked afraid to leave the door to order her off.

She wondered if the king had guards on the other walls, to
protect against sorcerers. Her enchantments would not get her
in that way—as if it held anything she had any desire to steal.
She could not sell any such thing and flee court with the money.
As for using anything. . . .

Maya remembered the sword, glittering gold and sapphire by
the candlelight, and froze. For all the gilt, it was a true sword,
made of gold and sapphire because no wizard could make an
uncommon sword out of common metal. Her tongue touched
her lip. The traitor's rose could only break enchantments.

She forced her breath in and out. The guards eyed her as if
about to decide that her standing there was more dangerous than
their leaving the door to see her off. She had to disarm them, get
within, and get that sword. . . .

Her gaze played over them. Once the gryphon was free—and
she could hear voices and other stirrings, the court was coming

awake—these men would die as soon as someone called for the guard. Her hands rose. For the first time in her life, Maya cast enchantments on men.

They still stared at her. As, indeed, they would, if enchanted. Her heart hammering, Maya walked forward, took the keys from the captain with polite thanks, and went to unlock the door. Even remembering she had taken the keys without resistance could not calm her as she turned her back on them to do it, but the guards did not move as she turned the key and opened the door.

The room gleamed, and she inched within. A jumble of gold and jewels—but on top lay the sword, sheathed and not glittering. Maya snatched it up. After an unsteady moment, she put two hands to it, awkward though that was with the keys in hand.

Outside, she locked the door, gave back the keys, told the guards to not remember that she had taken the sword, and walked off. Once out of sight, she broke the enchantment before another thief broke in.

Then she ran.

Noise sounded ahead: courtiers' chatter. She would need to enchant at least the guards, to get into the garden. Her mouth tightened. How easy it was, once you cast that first enchantment on men, to cast the second—

Screams broke into her thoughts. She ran faster.

Courtiers spilled out, women tripping over skirts, men colliding with pillars, in their haste. Maya slid by the walls, keeping the sword close by her. The milling crowds burst by, making her stagger on occasion, but soon, they left her path open. She ran again, with her heart hammering in fear.

At the door to the garden, guards, white as bone, peered within, glanced about the outside, held their swords in hand. Maya made out people still within as she ran up.

Guards turned, their swords rising, and Maya cast the enchantment faster than she had ever cast anything before. Leaving the dazed men behind, she darted through the gate.

Green everywhere, with white court clothing—Maya's gaze went to red, saw it was a rosebush, and went on. Behind a thicket, she heard noises. She drew the sword, cast away the scabbard, and moved through the garden.

Bodies, marred with red, lay about the gryphon, with its beak and forepaws bloodied. It screamed at King Karlon, and a couple of courtiers, who tried to ward it off with swords. Maya had barely time to see it was golden from beak to the tip of its tail, and register that more enchantments than hers had broken. The sword weighed in her hands, calling her thoughts back.

Maya ran past the thicket. The gryphon's side faced her, and she drove the sword in. The blade cut through hide and flesh, and blood fountained, splattering Maya. She leapt back, and the gryphon screamed, its head whipping about to face her. She raised the blood-covered sword and wondered if she could possibly parry that beak—if anyone could. It screamed again, more weakly, raising a paw. The blood flowing out its side was neither so fierce nor so brilliant a shade of red as when she first struck.

Maya scuttled back. Her feet collided with a step, and she went sprawling. She thought of rising and, instead, rolled away, landing in a flower bed.

At that, when the gryphon collapsed and sprawled over the ground, its beak came within inches of her foot.

The gryphon did not move, and Maya did not breathe. Then it sighed and lay still. Maya eyed it and steadied her breath for a long minute, with a pungent scent of crushed plants not managing to drown out the blood, before she even dare try to rise.

She managed on her first try, but then she merely stood, feeling vague, holding the sword loosely. Some sprawled bodies still bled brilliantly red, and servants moved to help them, but some bodies would never stir again.

The two nearest the gryphon were Lady Tatyana and Lord Dariko. She had fallen so that her arm lay over his body. Wide puddles of dark red blood spread against the green. More oozed out to join the puddle, but not much, and slowly.

"I beg your pardon, Mistress Maya."

King Karlon looked her mourning up and down, and Maya knew the news had to be bad: apologizing to a mere poor relation?

She kept her head bowed.

"There is a law—a sovereign law—that decrees whoever causes a death can not inherit from the dead."

Maya froze. She had not even considered how few relatives Lord Dariko had.

"Since your enchantments gave Lord Dariko the confidence to bring the gryphon out of the menagerie—I must declare that your acts resulted in his death."

Maya forced her breath in and out. How could it hurt so much to lose an inheritance she had not known of?

She managed to speak, precisely, and truthfully enough: "I can see why."

"A sad thing, after your service, but my hands are bound." He folded them together. "Indeed, I would permit a decent interval for grief before broaching the matter, but by law, the decrees must be made, by name, within seven days of the death—to prevent the impudence of false heirs."

"Registered by the council of nobles and all?" said Maya, dryly.

"Even so. So I must act at once. I grieve to spring this upon you in your bereavement."

Maya considered who Lord Dariko's heir might be, now. She had her suspicions, but it could be someone of whom King Karlon desired a favor.

She raised her head. "You swore at your coronation to uphold the law."

King Karlon eyed her.

"The king is under the law, for it is the law that makes him king."

"Ah, you understand my duty—I will, of course, ensure that all of Lord Dariko's household are taken on."

Maya nodded, knowing who the heir was. He would have the clerks search formally, of course, and be surprised as anyone, to curb the accusations he could not stay, but he knew.

"The cats should probably be sold." Maya glared at the white wolf. "The courtiers would no doubt pay good coin to have their mice caught *elegantly*."

"We can't sell them," said a nervous man-servant, "we—the heir might want—something else." He waved his hand.

"Best to have notions in hand when the heir arrives," said Maya, severely, "so we can tell him. You *know* how quickly a servant should be ready to serve his master." A poor relation should be as ready, she thought. Even if the clerks had already taken a month, pothering about in search of the proper heir.

"How well you know your duties, Maya." King Karlon's voice rang through the menagerie. She curtseyed. Servants bowed about her. "You are here to help?"

"It is part of Lord Dariko's estate," said Maya. "It should not fall to ruin while clerks determine his heir." It gives me something to do, she thought; I could let it go awry, and lie about what happened; the heir would not be able to tell.

"Certainly," said the king. "A *jewel* of his estate. The heir will be quite fond of it—no doubt."

Servants looked puzzled, as if they had not guessed who the heir was.

"Sire!" A clerk bowed in the doorway and eyed the birds. "The matters of the inheritance have been settled."

"Good man!" said King Karlon. "Let me hear them."

The clerk eyed the servants and Maya.

"This news will spread over the court," said the king, grandly. "The instant the heirs are known, every courtier will desire their names—and there is no reason to keep them in ignorance of who the heirs are."

"There are not *heirs*, Sire," said the clerk. The king blinked. "Lord Dariko predeceased Lady Tatyana. She was his nearest kin after—" He glanced nervously at Maya. "She inherited for moments before her own death."

"Dear me," said King Karlon, slowly. "I had not realized they were so closely akin."

"It was a hard hunt through marriages, births, and deaths. But Lady Tatyana was his heir, and her heir receives all."

"So—the heir. The courtiers will prize that knowledge still more. Who is this heir?"

"Mistress Maya," said the clerk, briskly.

The clerk might as well have spoken in a foreign tongue. Maya blinked. She knew of no one else named Maya, in court or out of it.

"Don't be absurd." King Karlon spoke sharply, but his face was pale. "If she caused Lord Dariko's death, she caused Lady Tatyana's death and can not inherit."

"Sire, the decree must be made *by name*. It was made by name, for *Lord Dariko*—and the seven days are up. By law, Mistress Maya can not be debarred from inheriting. Such is the law."

King Karlon opened and shut his mouth, like a fish out of water.

Maya let her breath out slowly. She knew him. King Karlon would have a plan within minutes. The king and courtiers were more dangerous to her than the gryphon, and she had less time to act—to win her escape from their attempt to tame her.

Unless—she straightened.

"*Mistress* Maya?" she said, icily. "Is there not a title attached to these estates?"

Birds fluttered about her. The clerk turned, slowly.

"I understand that in such troubled times, you are thinking of other matters. But I would not wish you to—fall into a bad habit."

The clerk bowed more deeply than he had to the king. "Lady Maya. Your graciousness toward this humble clerk is cherished."

Maya nodded. Servants looked at her with large eyes, and she let her breath out. She had to assure them that she was casting off no one. Sell off the menagerie. Put all the inheritance in order. But first—

Maya looked at the king. "I must see to my estate. And I do not know how such a gawky, rawboned noblewoman as I would make a courtier—with eyes like a cow's, no less." When King Karlon's face turned even paler, she suppressed a smile. "No matter. I must see to my estate, first."

She stalked away, like a wild lioness.

Over the Sea to Me

Seamstresses twittered over Beichan's torn shirt, their voices rising from about his knees, since not one of them rose as high as his waist. Most had dark hair and lined faces like dried apples, but some had birds' heads, with sharp beaks and feathers under their shawls instead of hair—he drew in a deep breath, to steady himself. Living at this castle for ten months should have left him used to its marvels.

"We should dye it back to blue," said one, eyeing him. "Yellow hair and blue eyes aren't enough to win the ladies." He looked away, sharply, and felt his face heat.

"Sir Beichan!" The chamberlain's voice boomed up the stairs. The little nut-brown chamberlain hopped after it, his berry-red coat sweeping the steps like a train. A strange knight, behind him, eyed the chamberlain as if not quite believing, though he managed to climb.

The seamstresses peered at the knight with bright-eyed interest.

"Sir Adkyn entered King Thomas's service." The chamberlain tilted his head back. "You twain will share a room."

Sir Adkyn eyed the seamstresses.

"Hadn't you heard, sir?" said the chamberlain. "Before you came? How the queen came over the sea in a ship of ivory?"

With a crew of hobs and sprites, thought Beichan. Who stayed and served her, and now her widower, and her daughter. He kept his mouth from twitching. Like any young knight who sought service with foreign kings, he had looked for marvels. He found them. Often, other knights had found them entirely too marvelous.

"I had heard," said Sir Adkyn, flatly.

He looked eager to be gone, and kept only by his oath—King Thomas would no doubt free him within a month or two, with a contemptuous smile, but until then—Beichan bowed.

"I will show you where the room lies."

The chamberlain grinned. "I will have his luggage lugged there." He hopped down the stairs, his coat tail flying.

Beichan turned back to the seamstresses. "There is no need to take special care with it. I wear that when I need clothes that can get filthy without trouble."

"You've got no surety that ladies will not see you then," said a seamstress merrily, and ran off with the shirt flapping like a banner. Beichan sighed and turned back to Sir Adkyn.

Wind blew through the windows as they walked down the corridor, bearing the smell of the sea, and an almost wintry nip to the air.

Adkyn said, "Strange servants in this castle."

"You hadn't heard of them before?" said Beichan.

"I heard rumors. Which—" Adkyn shook his head. "I did not believe them, which was wise. This castle and its servants are much more than rumor said."

That, Beichan remembered himself. "When I came—there were fae lasses, no higher than my waist, frolicking on the seashore." He shook his head and glanced at Adkyn. Wild little things, brown like driftwood, their hair wild and their arms like twigs, wearing sea blue gowns, cheerful and laughing—but Adkyn had no wish to be regaled by the story.

He pushed open the door to a small, white-washed room, with a single window like an arrow slit that gave enough light to see two beds and two chests, and the empty candle sconce on the wall. Beichan, gesturing at the other, sat on his own bed. Adkyn sat with obvious relief, though they had not walked far, and his gaze darted about the chamber, as if assuring himself that none of the fae were here.

Within a minute, a grinning brown hob, half the chamberlain's height, walked into the room, balancing bags five times its size in its shoulder. Adkyn winced. The hob landed them beside his bed, bowed deeply, perhaps more deeply than a human could, and left.

Adkyn said, heavily, "Not all the tales can be true."

"More than you think." Beichan pointed at a knothole in the wall. "The servant who keeps this room sometimes pops out of that."

Adkyn eyed him. Annoyance stung at Beichan. If he had heard the tales, he should have come for them, not in belief he would not find them.

"He does not duck his head to sweep under the beds, either. Serving here makes a bolder tale than any other king you could serve."

"*You* seem content with it."

Beichan laughed. "Men said I would not last a month, but I have already served ten."

A brown hob, no higher than Beichan's knee, walked along the hallway past their room; she wore a gown of patches, in red, green, and brown, and lugged a laundry basket seven times her size. She caroled merrily.

"Are there other humans here?" said Adkyn, as in despair.

Beichan laughed again; he could not help himself. "There are other knights. Some have served here seven years and more. And King Thomas has a daughter, and she has her ladies. They are as human as you and I." He went to the window. "Look."

Narrow though it was, the window showed an apple tree, flowering white in the shelter of the garden walls, and Lady Isobel sitting beneath it, her gown as gray as a rainy cloud, and her hair golden. Next to her, in brilliant scarlet, a hob stood; his head did not reach as high as hers.

"The hob's her chamberlain, but there's Lady Isobel herself."

Adkyn eyed the scene. Laughter floated up.

"Since the King's Grace does not require us," said Beichan, "gallant knights would attend the ladies."

Sir Beichan left with a light step. Adkyn followed, down flights of stairs through the stones still chilled with winter, to an oaken door. Opened, the door let in the scent of spring flowers and the warmer air, where the walls sheltered it from wind.

Beichan gathered white violets from the lawn and approached Lady Isobel. From the doorway, Adkyn watched. He had thought, up in the chamber—and thought rightly. No wonder Beichan could endure those eerie hobs; no wonder those uncanny seamstresses chortled over his shirt. Lady Isobel was a fair maiden, with golden hair and a lily white face. But even in a plain gray gown, she was the king's daughter. Only a fool would forget it.

Lady Isobel took the flowers, laughing. Adkyn's eyes narrowed. Then, that yellow-haired Beichan was a handsome young man. Lady Isobel might prove fool enough to forget it herself.

A man who served King Thomas well might receive a good reward, even if his service was short. Adkyn looked away. He knew whose son Beichan was. Of high birth to enter service, even if he desired adventure. High enough to dream—

"Sir Adkyn!" Beichan called. Isobel looked, with clear gray eyes. The breeze tossed pale petals about their heads.

Adkyn bowed. He served King Thomas, not Lady Isobel, certainly not Sir Beichan.

Outside the narrow windows, the sky showed purple and black on the thick western clouds, and the air even in the castle grew colder. King Thomas sat by the blazing fireplace, where the cold was least, and its orange color flickered on his face. "You have served me a fortnight, Sir Adkyn. How do you find my castle?"

Adkyn went on one knee on the stone floor and offered the goblet of red wine, the gold and ruby glinting in the firelight, the draught itself a somber crimson in shadow. The king took the goblet, but Adkyn did not rise.

"I find your castle pleasant, Your Grace, and your service an honor. I have also learned of a matter you might be glad to learn of."

The king's eyes narrowed. Firelight glittered on them.

"Your Grace might be well-advised to watch closely while Sir Beichan attends your daughter."

The words slid from the king's mouth like a breeze in the trees. "My—daughter—"

Adkyn bent his head and even so fought down his smile, to keep his face as grave and smooth as befit a knight having to warn the king of such a danger.

Breezes had sent the apples' petals far and wide, but daffodils bloomed, for new color, and in the sun-warmed air, Isobel sat with her ladies. A lady played a lute, and Isobel and Beichan bent their heads over a game of draughts.

On the ramparts, the wind blew and smelled of salt. The garden flowered as it did only in the walls' shelter.

"Look at them," said King Thomas. "My daughter in an embroidered gown. And Sir Beichan, a scarlet tunic, and scarlet shoes, as if for a feast."

Adkyn nodded.

"They play the game slowly, do they not?" said King Thomas.

Lady Isobel moved a piece.

"That they do," Adkyn said.

Isobel laughed, and King Thomas's mouth tightened.

"This is not *quite* the game that my mother brought over the sea," said Isobel. Her finger brushed one of the delicate ivory coins, engraved with a rose. "One by one, each piece has broken or been lost, to be replaced."

Beichan moved a piece. "Hard to believe that each one came from a different hand at a different time."

Isobel giggled. "By one hand, at least. He was—" Her mouth stopped, her face composed itself, and she rose. Isobel's ladies curtseyed, and without needing to look back and see who had entered the garden, Beichan rose to bow.

"I grieve to disturb you, my lady," King Thomas said to Isobel, "but I must bring my knight away."

Beichan bowed again. "I am in your service, Your Grace," he said, but felt chilled at this urgency, as if a dragon or an army had come to menace the realm. He bowed to Isobel in farewell and hurried after King Thomas without a glance back. A messenger might have come with ill news, and he had taken service to fight the king's foes, not to sit in the garden.

He did not know the halls they walked down. Wood gave way to stone, and no window opened into the chilly corridor— not even arrow slits. Their way was lit and warmed only by torches.

When he saw locked doors, Beichan faltered. The dungeons. And though the servants were not human, they gossiped. He would have heard of any prisoner brought to the castle.

Two figures appeared, ahead—green, not brown. They barely reached to King Thomas's shoulder, but they were broad and muscled, their faces brutish, and their mouths held tusks like a wild boar's. They stood with spears, ready to attack.

King Thomas turned. His eyes were narrowed. "Give me your sword, Sir Beichan."

Beichan did not even breathe. He had served King Thomas loyally and in good faith.

"You might be stricken from knighthood for this, Sir Beichan. To seduce your liege lord's maiden daughter—"

Beichan's mouth opened.

"All that saves your life is your silence. I will hear no lies of innocence." The king's eyes narrowed. "Your sword."

The ogres lifted their spears. With those arms, a single thrust would tear through him.

Everyone in this castle served King Thomas and would not help him. Even if they would defy the king, they were too far off; he could not have roused aid even by shouting.

And he himself had sworn to serve this king.

His hands felt almost numb, but he felt an odd pride: he did his duty, and the king failed in his. He unbuckled his belt and handed King Thomas his sword.

The king jerked his head to one side. One ogre drew out a ring of keys and opened a door to a narrow, windowless room. It held neither straw nor chains, but another door stood on the wall opposite. The ogre opened that door as well; heavier, it moved more slowly. Behind it stood a room with a third door, the wood black with age. The ogre turned the keys on the ring. They rang as they fell against each other.

Nausea twisted Beichan's stomach. He should protest his innocence and die cleanly rather than molder here.

He opened his mouth. The other ogre struck him, knocking his breath from him. He staggered into the cell. Straw lay in one corner. High on the wall, a tiny window let in sunlight, but he could not see outside.

A chain sprawled across the stones. Beichan gagged. The ogres had the shackle about his ankle in moments, and King

Thomas nodded. The ogres bowed, a misshapen gesture, and withdrew.

The king stayed, beyond Beichan's reach. "Expect no rescue, Sir Beichan. Neither man nor fae can rescue a prisoner from my power."

The king withdrew without a glance back at him. The ogres returned, with a bowl of porridge, a pitcher of water, and a stool. Generosity, he thought, as they slammed one door and then the next. He could even hear the third door shut from the force. He shut his eyes and fancied he could hear the key in the lock.

He smelled the porridge. He shuddered and wondered if his stomach could endure food, but he opened his eyes.

Something skittered among the straw.

Beichan's gaze jerked over it. The shadows were too deep for him to see, but mice and rats would eat what he did not.

He dropped to his knees by the bowl. The porridge tasted like wood in his mouth, and more than once, he had to wash it down with water, but it quelled his stomach.

And then he sat on the stool, the chain rattling from his motion, and wondered how slowly the hours would pass.

He had lost all track of time, when light shone on the wall. The sun had descended far enough to shine into the cell. Beichan shuddered. King Thomas would not relent before nightfall. Or even, though summer and fall still lay ahead, before winter; the window would let in snow, and he doubted the ogres would fetch blankets for him.

He should sleep now, he thought. Rats and mice would like the night better.

"Lady Isobel!" called Jeanne. "You will take a chill, sitting by the window."

"A minute," Isobel said. In the courtyard, her father gave that new knight, Sir Adkyn, a goshawk. A knightly gift, but after less than a month's service?

She had not heard what grave matter taken Sir Beichan from the game. He had not returned, even to apologize. Why did her father give gifts, to men who had barely served him, when such matters, urgent and dire, were afoot? Why were none of the other knights sent as well?

A groom led a horse from the stable, and Sir Adkyn strode toward it. Her breath sighed out as she turned away.

The great chamber gleamed with candlelight; the sunny day had left it warmer than it commonly was, this early in spring, and the tiny flames only added to the heat. Knights served them on bended knee. While the knights could hear, Isobel only eyed her father with sideways glances.

With the pudding served, Isobel wet her lips with her wine and said, "I thought I saw Sir Adkyn leave."

"I fear so," said King Thomas. "He served me well."

"I have not seen Sir Beichan lately."

"You must not have seen him leave." King Thomas ate.

His cool voice gave her pause. After a moment, she said, "It is only fitting that a king be attended by servants of proper degree."

For a minute, King Thomas neither ate nor spoke. Then he said, "You are dear to consider it, my daughter, but do not trouble yourself."

She ate, though her stomach roiled. She would not trouble herself about his servants, indeed.

Sunset cast orange light on the cell when Beichan woke again. The straw made a poor bed; the stones left him stiff. He lay back and watched the orange deepen to scarlet, and that to crimson. The air grew colder about him. He had slept ill, thrashing through endless fancies of what he might have done, what King Thomas might have said, how Lady Isobel might have acted differently.

Not Isobel. Nothing that King Thomas could have said would have convinced him that Isobel had betrayed him. The king must have known that; he had not even tried.

Or perhaps—Beichan shifted—he had not cared. What did it matter what a prisoner thought of why he was imprisoned?

A skittering sounded, through the straw. Beichan's head jerked up. A shadow, smaller than his thumb, scurried over the stones. Beichan shuddered and cast about for the stool. Near his hand, a shrill cry sprung from the shadows. He grabbed the stool and sat. Lying on stone would leave every inch of him exposed.

Crimson slid into violet, and his ears strained the air for skittering mice and rats. Violet deepened into black.

A chuckle came through the cell—softly, from a mouth near the floor. Beichan gagged. It would be like this castle to have mice that jeered.

Nothing stirred. His eyes made out dim forms; then, the moon was full, and some light would trickle in, this night.

Chortles came from three or four mouths. "Aye, you seen something—new—here." Tiny footsteps pattered. Moonlight fell on one figure; though it was none too bright, Beichan saw a human form, no larger than his hand.

More or less human. Beichan prayed that the moonlight tricked his eyes. Skittering footsteps—but that might be mice, so small were the feet.

"Something new in the dungeon," said a voice by his feet. "Sent by our lord the king." Something jabbed at his ankle, like a mouse-sized sword. "We should not make his *sojourn* easy. A criminal deserves harshness."

Moonlight seeped into the cell. By it, Beichan saw figures no larger than his hand. Their faces and bodies were more twisted than the ogres', and their eyes glittered with avidity. Spriggans, Beichan thought.

"We should not sit and watch." One spriggan crept closer. "Not while this malcontent sits at leisure." His hand struck at Beichan's chained leg with bruising force.

Beichan lunged and seized him in one hand. The spriggan yelped and wrestled, and Beichan tightened his grip.

Screams of anger resounded in the cell. Spriggans descended on him. Two leapt to seize his fingers, about his captive; others struck and kicked—trying to distract. He had to clench his teeth to keep them from succeeding, but he hurled his first attacker across the room. Two spriggans still clung to his fingers; he shook them off. They hit the stones, but he barely heard the fall as the other spriggans assaulted him. He tried to stomp on one, but the chain clanked, and he could not move his foot quickly enough.

A spriggan laughed, shrilly, and Beichan moved his other foot, kicking it into the wall. The others roared in their tiny voices, and attacked.

A long time later, grumbling every inch, the spriggans retreated. Aching, Beichan sat on the stool and breathed hard. If they returned, this or any night—he fought down a groan, for fear that they would hear. They had beaten him black and blue. He did not know how long he could withstand them.

His hands formed fists again. They would have to overcome him, even if he could not fight them off. He had endured this night, even when he doubted his ability to.

He had to sleep by day, as best he could. He buried his face in hands. God have mercy on him, it would be harder with these bruises than with all that had plagued him the day before.

Drizzle dripped from the roof, but Billy Blind stood brightly beside her. "Cloth is needed, to keep your new ladies in fitting dress."

"I trust your judgment." Isobel glanced at the books on the table, the sums written in Billy Blind's neat hand. "You keep a wise eye on all the castle."

Billy Blind closed one eye and looked at her with the other, opening it wider than any human eye could open.

Isobel let her breath out. He knew her too well.

"Did you mark Sir Beichan's departure? I saw Sir Adkyn leave, but not Sir Beichan, and there was no reason for stealth."

"Didn't see Sir Beichan go," said Billy Blind.

"Did you see him come? Mark his horse?" Isobel glanced at the books and back at him. "Could you know it in the stables?"

"Know it in the stables? Of course not, my lady! Not because I wouldn't know it, a fine chestnut it was, but they will not stand it." He wagged his head. "No, no, not at all. I do not let grooms to trifle with my work. Proud fellows—they will not let me venture to the stables."

Drizzle hardened into rain, audible on the roof. Far off, thunder rumbled. Isobel sighed. Today, she could not, either. She had no excuse to be in the stables.

Mice skittered around the empty bowl. How the ogres chortled to find him asleep when they came with his meal, it seemed never to grow old with them, but at least they woke him before nightfall.

Beichan looked at the window. Again, the light on the wall gleamed scarlet. The night after King Thomas had imprisoned him, the moon had been full. Which meant, night by night, it had risen later and shed less light. Some nights, even that light had been lessened by clouds and rain. His bruises and the chain had not been the only hindrances he faced.

Beichan heard a giggle behind him. His eyes narrowed. A spriggan's footsteps were hard to pick out, but by not even breathing, he heard a spriggan approach.

Closer and closer—and then his hand dived downward, snatching. Something small and sharp pierced his hand, but he did not hesitate; his hand went around the body, and he hurled it away. The spriggan thudded against the stone, and something rang against the floor—more like a needle than a sword.

His hand still stung from its bite.

"Shows you," jeered another voice. "He's a brute—not to be shown down by one spriggan, but by all together."

The sky held great puffs of clouds, but white ones, and the air was already warm; her ladies could not plead the weather; at least, she would not let them. Not when she knew no more of Beichan than when he had left the garden.

"The weather is too fine to abide indoors," said Isobel. "We must go maying."

"Maying, my lady?" said Marguerite. "It will be too hot to gather flowers by noon."

Isobel smiled, as if she donned a mask. "Then we should go at once—I am already wearing my green gown—you should ready yourselves."

The ladies scrambled to obey.

Isobel rose. "I will order the grooms ready horses."

"My lady!" squealed Jeanne. "It is not proper—"

"Then you must hurry to follow," said Isobel. She rushed down the stairs, her skirts gathered in her hands to clear her feet, so that none of them could follow in time. At the stables, she

called the head groom. The man bowed and promised the
spirited mounts.

"No," said Isobel, "we only go maying—" She stepped past
him, into the stables. The air smelled of straw and horse, and she
let her eyes adjust. She spoke of gentle mounts, and how her
ladies could not all ride well; she did not know how she managed,
while eyeing the horses.

When she saw Beichan's chestnut, words clogged in her
mouth.

The head groom hustled her out, making promises. Isobel
went. She swallowed, remembering the day Beichan had rode
into this courtyard, the way her ladies had once again giggled over
a handsome new knight, and their guesses at how long it would
take him to leave. . . .

Her hands formed fists. Whatever her father's madness had
been, she did not doubt he was cunning. He had hidden
Beichan's fate from her; she would hide her knowledge from him.

In the courtyard, her ladies hurried up. "You should have
waited," said Marguerite.

"See, we were not long," said Jeanne.

"And now," said Isobel, "the horses won't be long." A breeze
carried the sea scent by her, and tugged at her skirt and hair. She
would be ill company, gathering flowers, when all her thoughts
would rove back to what had befallen Beichan.

Marguerite opened her mouth to chide again, and the grooms
started to lead out the horses.

Relieved, Isobel went to hers. At least, she thought, the ride
and the flowers would hide her mood. But as they rode through
grass that lashed at their legs and paused to gather blooms, and
clouds thickened, her ladies whispered.

Some even said, "With Sir Beichan gone, she does not find the
maying sweet."

The third time she heard that, half-sick with the thought they would bear such talk to her father, Isobel said, "It is not, after all, the heat that is to be feared, but the rain. We must ride back."

The ladies shrugged; they had baskets filled with flowers, and garlands. She carried garlands of her own, petals of gold and pale blue spilled from her lap, but her thoughts were intent on how she could learn—

The dungeon.

Isobel let her breath out. She was a fool. Beichan had not left, and no one gossiped of him. The only place he could lie without tongues wagging was the dungeon. Seamstresses prattled of how closemouthed the jailors were.

You did not *know* that, Isobel told herself, her gaze going ahead, to where the castle sat on the shore, and their horses clopped toward it.

Before the clouds grew much thicker, they rode through the gate. A groom handed her down, and with her ladies, she went to the solar, climbing the stairs while only half aware of them. There she sewed, stabbing the cloth when she remembered it, letting it lie when she forgot. The ladies murmured again.

"My lady." said Marguerite. "Your sewing!"

Isobel tossed the cloth aside. "You are right to rebuke me. It is wicked of me. I will go to the chapel and pray God to mend my ways." She left before the ladies could propose following her.

Her heart hammered as she went down the stairs, and her prayers rose in earnest: that they would not follow her. That no one would notice her, or how she took the path by the dungeons, where its windows that let on the grassy courtyard.

His hand burned.

Beichan stared at the gloom. Day shed little light; it had lessened as the hours passed, and his hand worsened. Though the ogres were none too lavish with the pitcher, he had sacrificed water to wash his wound. Still, his hand burned and ached. He sat on the floor, leaning on the stool he could not trust himself to sit on.

His state would please the spriggans.

He laid his head on the stool. He had barely rested that day; his fevered thoughts would not be still. Neither man nor fae would rescue him, King Thomas said.

No man—or woman?

He shifted. Straw crackled under him.

His voice sounded dream-like in his own ears. "If any woman were to rescue me—If any old widow rescued me, I would serve her as a son. If any wife rescued me, I would serve her as a knight. If any maiden rescued me—" He stirred himself, sat up. Visions of Isobel danced in his thoughts: grave over the game, listening to a lute by the fire, sitting at the high table with her father for a feast. "I would make her my wife with a golden ring, and make her lady of all my lands, the towers of Linn. . . ."

It stabbed like a sword: he would never see either towers or lands again. His father would never learn what became of him. He closed his eyes.

Despite the clouds, despite the candles flickering within, it was darker within the chapel than without. Isobel stood, breathing hard from her hurry, and thought that she should pray. Her gaze flickered about the walls, to see the saints depicted in icons. Though they showed neither color nor brightness, she picked out St. Roch, St. Dominic, St. Valentine. Her breath eased, and she could hear how her heart pounded as her thoughts assembled and found order. The patrons of prisoners, of the falsely accused—of lovers—she shuddered. The moment she had known what her father had done, and realized that Beichan sounded ill and fevered.

She had thought of calling to Beichan, but only briefly; she could have been heard. She swallowed, and her gaze went down to the crucifix. Her father would never have imprisoned a man and lied about his leaving if he had had just reason to punish him. Not even another king's son could hope to be avenged against him

For an unjust cause though—and she knew he had one—he had never tried to arrange her marriage, and had done much to discourage wooers.

She heard footsteps on the path outside, and rushed forward. If they found her just standing here, they would bustle her back, chiding about how she did not pray.

And she had much to pray for. Save her, no one in the castle could help Beichan.

Supper was over, but—Isobel glanced out the window—it would be long hours yet until nightfall. She looked back at her sewing. Beichan had lived for days in the dungeon. She had to wait out the hours until darkness would hide her, and hope that it would not prove fatal.

She rose. "I am going to the distillery."

"Is anything needed?" said Marguerite.

"No servants has brought a message about medicines," said Jeanne, as quickly.

"Perhaps a sleeping posset," said Isobel, "that I might sleep better."

She did not hear the soft words behind her as she slipped out the door. Then, she did not need to; she padded down the corridor, knowing that they would talk of how she needed it, with her restlessness, and marvel about how she had fretted all the more since she had gone to the chapel, and rejoice that the distillery was farther in, so that they did not need to escort her.

Isobel was glad of that, when she compounded the posset in the distillery. They would wonder about how many herbs she used, and how large a brew she cooked. She sighed. She could hardly tell them what she had heard, while going to the chapel.

Finally, she set it to cool, and went in search of Billy Blind.

When she found him on a stairway, he said, "My lady, I am sorry to hear that you are restive today."

Isobel sat on the stone steps, putting their heads on level. "I just made a sleeping posset. So my ladies will not worry if I wander tonight."

Billy Blind blinked.

"Now, the ogres, the jailers. I know they will not drink anything given to them—"

His eyes widened like plates, but Billy Blind nodded.

She let her breath out. He had come over the sea to be her mother's chamberlain, and now he was hers; without so loyal a servant, she could do nothing.

"Give them a roast pig or the like. They will not realize that the sauce holds a sleeping posset, not if I know them." She smiled a little. "My mother taught me to oversee a kitchen. I will sauce it myself."

She thought. "I will need other things." She marshaled a list. If Billy Blind told her it could not be done tonight, she would have to defer it, but Beichan had sounded—she did not wish to leave him there a night more than she needed to. Her mouth tightened. She did not wish to leave him an hour more, but she needed nightfall.

There was no moon. She was glad of that.

Abed, Isobel stared at the ceiling and tried to master her breathing. The single night candle gave little light, but the ladies had to sleep. If any of them saw her—she had given them some of the posset, but disguised in a nightcap, and split between so many—

Marguerite snored.

Isobel eased herself from beneath the blankets and, in the chilly night air, pulled her bedrobe over her shift. She could not take the candle.

For a moment, she looked with longing at her shoes. She had time enough to don them. But, shod, she could not steal past her father's bedchamber. At least, she could not risk it.

She padded from the room, barely breathing, and did not fully shut the door; the lock would click. But it closed off the candlelight, and she stood in the starlit gloom—for no more than a moment, as her eyes adjusted.

She turned.

In the starlight, though little more than a shape of gray, Billy Blind nodded, solemnly. Isobel let her breath out. He could speak no more than she could, but as he had carried out her orders—even the horse, which must have been hard—all was well.

She stole toward the stairs. Billy Blind vanished. Then, his part was done; her was not. She started down the stairs. She could not run. Even barefoot, she would wake someone.

She slipped across the great chamber, where night breezes brushed her with coldness, down stairs again, and into the great hall. There, a side door let her into a gallery. Glad she did not have to risk the length of the great hall, Isobel walked along it. Outside, an owl hooted. She walked more quickly. Even approaching the door, she slowed, but she did not stop.

Inside, the torches shone brightly, where they did not wait for day. Isobel stopped to listen. The echoes of the ogres' snores resounded. She shivered in the stony cold and crept down the stone corridor, about a turn, down another, and about a second turn. There, a greenish foot stuck out into the corridor.

She barely breathed, coming up to the door. One ogre sprawled in the doorway; he did not carry the keys. Inside, the other snored, his head on the table. Pig bones lay scattered in the straw, and herbs from the posset teased her nose, though, in the filth, if she had not known of them, she would never have recognized the smell.

Isobel stepped over the ogre's leg, into the room. The torches cast more shadows than light. If the room had held more than the table and stools, she could not have managed, but she picked her way about the table and bones. The keys glinted on the ogre's belt.

She went to one knee and, more delicately than she had ever sewed a stitch, unfastened the keys.

They clanked against each other, one ogre shifted, and her heart leapt. She did not even try to retreat, and reminding herself of the sleeping posset's potency did nothing to calm her. Her heart hammered out the minutes until the ogre snored again, and she dared step back. The other ogre had rolled over and lay squarely in the door. She drew a deep breath and stepped over his waist, and into the hall.

Then through the corridors, her heart in her throat, and down stairs, calculating doors, fighting to keep from running. She remembered the window where she had heard Beichan's lament and his—her face heated—promise. But she had to find it from the inside.

Finally, she stopped before the door. She had counted as best she could; she sorted through the keys. Several failed her, but one clicked in, and the door slid open. The second door made her blink. She glanced behind herself and eased toward it. It, too, made her search for the key but opened easily.

At the third door, she quailed. She should have asked Billy Blind to sccut the dungeons as well. She looked at the keys. The torchlight barely reached far enough to make them gleam.

Something sounded behind that door. Isobel looked up. Perhaps a moan—her tongue touched her lips. When a high-pitched giggle followed, she tried key after key in the lock; one turned in the lock, and she threw open the door.

Even this far from its source, the torchlight fell across the floor. A man lay there, face-down, only his yellow hair visible; even the side of his face was hidden by his arm. About him, tiny figures lurked. Her shadow fell on them. They cringed away, their distorted faces turning toward the light.

Spriggans, she thought. "How dare you!" she shouted, not caring about ogres or fathers. They fled, vanishing into the shadows, and moments later, the rustle of straw also fell silent. She barely could care.

Isobel dropped to her knees. By their redness, she knew the clothes Beichan had worn when he vanished. Tattered, filthy, recognizable—she laid a hand to his arm.

A mouse skittered through the straw. Slowly, Beichan stirred and raised his face to look at her. His beard had grown—and been gnawed on by mice. His hair was ragged from the same cause. His face was flushed; she put a hand to his forehead and felt the heat.

Beichan raised his hand. "It was one—the spriggans." His mouth contorted. "A needle, I think."

She took his hand, and he winced. The hand was marred with redness almost as bright as his clothes had been, clean.

"I should have struck those spriggans," said Isobel. "I should have."

Beichan gave a puff of breath, which could have been a laugh. But, thought Isobel, the blow, however deserved, would have delayed Beichan's freedom. She looked about. The chain trailed over the straw from Beichan's ankle. She reached for the keys; moments later, she helped him to his feet.

She stuck the key in the last keyhole, and the key-ring jangled. Let her father consider *that*.

Billy Blind used this stark, windowless room for storage—but candles lit it, it was warmer, and it held no rats. Beichan lay, half-asleep, on a cot.

"I will need my mother's salve," said Isobel. "The one she brought on the ship."

Billy Blind nodded and headed toward the door.

"I should leave," said Beichan, not quite opening his eyes. "Once you tend me—to beyond your father's grasp. And where he can not find that you aided me."

"You are not well enough," said Isobel. "And if you were, I can not give you a horse swift enough to outrun my father." She sat on a stool. "When he hunts for you, you can ride the other way. I have a horse for you, and gold, and—fitting gifts, for the service you have rendered my father."

"A comb for your hair," caroled Billy Blind, "a razor for your beard—myself as a barber." He plopped the salve by Isobel and swept a deep bow.

Isobel laughed. "Is there anything you do not do well, Billy Blind?"

"I make a very poor confectioner, my lady."

Isobel laughed again and took Beichan's hand. The wound was small, a needle stick, but hotter to the touch than his face. She smeared her mother's salve over it, and the hand seemed to cool beneath her fingers.

"It will not make you well at once," she said, softly. "You must rest for a day and an hour, to give it time."

She rubbed her eyes with the back of her hand. The night was passing. As if reminded, she yawned. "I have to go back. Before he wakes, I have to sleep. . . ."

"Go," said Beichan.

She lowered his hand and stood. She would sleep better now.

Enraged bellows woke her. Her face in the pillow, Isobel tried to reason out the sound.

When Jeanne pulled on her blankets, saying, "My lady!" she sat. Footsteps sounded in the hallways.

"My lady, your father—"

Isobel wondered how much sleep she had had. She felt as gray as the morning. Still—"Something is wrong." She rose before her bed lured her back. Her ladies fluttered about the door, but none of them reached for the latch. From the scrape of talons on the stone, the ogres came to the king.

Isobel raised her head. "Dress me."

The ladies scrabbled to fetch a gown. Isobel wished she could go back to bed. She held up her arms and let them dress her, and her mouth twisted. Even in bed, she had drowsed off, remembered Beichan lying on the stones, and jolted back to wakefulness; it was not only her rescuing him that had cost her sleep.

The women laced her up. She yawned.

"My lady?" said Jeanne.

"I—" said Isobel. The ladies looked at her. A half-truth, at least. "I slept badly last night—perhaps I brewed the posset wrong—"

"I dreamed," said young Eloise. "*Terrible* dreams."

The voices rose then; three-quarters of them claimed dreams of whatever evil had happened.

"We can attend to our sewing," said Isobel. "That will keep us honestly occupied and out of the way."

"My lady! Don't you want to *know*?"

Isobel straightened. "Not," she said, in as queenly a manner as she could, "if it distract the king my father from dealing with whatever evil has befallen us."

Completely out of the way, thought Isobel. They had nothing to do but sew and listen to the scrambling feet.

The Angelus bell chimed. Isobel bent her head to pray.

When she raised it again, Billy Blind stood beside her. "My lady, the fabric? For your ladies' gowns?"

For a moment, Isobel thought he tried to hint about Sir Beichan without alerting her ladies. Then, they had talked of cloth before. And she still had to clad her ladies.

"Not today, I fear. The rain would spot the cloth. When the weather clears, we must buy some. In scarlet and green, to make a brave show."

Billy Blind bowed.

"But stay by me." She had thought since last night. "I wondered—you came with my mother, and I have heard tales of that ship. That it was of gold—"

Billy Blind chortled. "No hob would tell you that. *Ivory*, with sails and ropes of silk."

Isobel nodded. Her mother had come over the sea to marry her father, but now she wanted to send a man away. "I wonder if that ship might bear others over the sea."

Billy Blind's eyebrows shot up. "It might, at *great* need. Folly to even try, if there were any other way."

Such as, by horseback, with a purse to buy passage. Isobel's mouth twisted, and she sewed a few more stitches.

The door opened. From the doorway, King Thomas smiled at her. At least, his mouth smiled. Her ladies pulled away.

"Good morning, Father." She was pleased with how clear she made her voice. "I hope that whatever evil it was has ended."

"You are close in conference with your chamberlain," said King Thomas.

"On cloth," said Isobel. "And how my mother came to this castle. Nothing fit to trouble you with, when such urgent matters are afoot."

His mouth twitched. Her ladies quailed.

"Some wretch stole the jailors' keys and freed a prisoner. Left the key ring in the lock so that I would not doubt it."

"Have you caught—him?" After a moment, she added, "Or was it a woman?"

"It was a man," said King Thomas, "and he fled the castle. You must wait to leave until my knights can protect you."

Her heart beat, not faster, but harder.

"He left within minutes," said Isobel. Her voice echoed in the stone corridor. "You could have summoned me then."

Billy Blind chuckled. "Your knight would *not* have liked that."

"I—" Isobel stepped inside the room, where Beichan sat on the stool. He wore new clothing, bright in blue and gold. Billy Blind had played the barber; Beichan was clean-shaven, and his hair lay more neatly—and darkly, being wet. Across the room, the tub still held water, and she felt her face heating.

Beichan looked up. Her breath caught. After a moment, she felt the color seeping from her face. Not everything had been grime. Little wonder he had shielded his face with his arm.

She came in quiet and composed, she saw that he was sitting and not lying abed, but still she paled.

Beichan surged to his feet. Isobel let her breath out as he moved, and some color came back into her face. He still took her hand and drew her over to the stool, and it did not take much urging before she sat.

Humming under his breath, Billy Blind hefted the tub, water and all, to his shoulder and carried it out.

Beichan let his breath out. "I fear I do not remember last night well. Did I thank you, my lady?"

"Sir Beichan, I did it to keep disgrace from my father's name." She did not look up at him.

"You faced danger for that, my lady? I do not know how many cells you opened—"

Isobel straightened. "I knew which cell you were in. You—at the window, I heard you, yesterday."

Well for him that she had listened yesterday. The days before, he had slept; yesterday, he had rambled in his fever. Then, he had not forgotten what he had said. And fevered or no, he had meant it.

"Your father said that neither man nor fae could rescue me," he said. Isobel looked at her hands, in her lap. "I was ready to reward any *woman* who would do it."

Isobel's hands clasped each other.

"A maiden who rescued me, I would make my wife and lady of my lands." Slowly, watching for withdrawal, Beichan reached for her hand. His was only inches from hers when she took it. He swallowed. Immured within this room, he could offer her nothing.

"I must win my way from your father's lands," he said. "Ride from the kingdom, take ship—a fortnight at best—"

Her voice was soft. "At the very best. The roads, the bridges—even your horse might fail you. Travelers have taken months." She drew a deep breath. "You may not be able to take ship before the winter storms come. You could be a year merely getting home."

"Still," he said, his voice pitched no more loudly than hers, "if you wish it, I will bring you with me."

She looked up. He could not read her face. His voice slowed.

"I would think it more fitting for so noble a lady to wait for me to return and bear her off, but it is not you who made a pledge to me."

Her voice was sweet. "I would be a burden to you as you escaped my father."

"Never!"

A chortle sounded from the doorway. Billy Blind swaggered in. "Do not expect him to talk like that forever, my lady. Lovers turn into husbands." He leaned against the wall. "Your father never talked like that to your mother after they had been wed a twelvemonth."

"He still loved her," said Isobel.

Billy Blind shrugged. "Didn't say he wouldn't love."

Isobel's gaze went down again.

"I will return," said Beichan. "Whatever happens, I will take you as my wife within—" Returning might take as long, or longer, than leaving. "—three years."

Her hand came out to take his. "And I will take you as my husband."

"Hurray!" caroled Billy Blind. "The words of marriage have been spoken; you are betrothed. You even have a witness, though two such noble souls would never forswear themselves."

Beichan pulled his hand away—no more quickly than Isobel did. From the heat in his face, he thought he blushed more red than she did.

"And," said Billy Blind, "her father hunts north with his men. I can point you south."

"And," said Isobel, rising, "you need not return as if my father threw you from his service. Sir Adkyn received a fine gift when he left; I will give you better. And a purse of gold to ease your way." She turned to a chest to draw out a horn of ivory, with a baldric of green. Like a fairy horn, Beichan thought, taking it from her hands. "And come—"

She sounded light-hearted again; he followed her down the corridor and heard dogs yapping. Hounds, silver and shaggy, surged up the stones and licked her face. Isobel laughed, patting their heads. "And a horse—I fear we can not restore to you the horse you rode here."

"The grooms are *jealous*," said Billy Blind. "They won't let me in the stable."

"But—a horse." Isobel led him on. Sleek and as silvery as the hounds, a horse looked up from hay.

"A *swift* horse," said Billy Blind. "You will be shipboard before King Thomas *hears* of this horse bearing you off." With his eyes like saucers, he glanced sideways at Beichan. "And King Thomas won't miss it for all his talk. . . ."

"His talk?" said Isobel, sharply.

Billy Blind's mouth pursed, his lips going farther than they had any business going. "He's talked, my lady. And the ogres have assured him that if Sir Beichan ran off, there's no danger that the fae of the castle will flit, with you and him."

"Oh," said Isobel.

"They came," said Beichan softly, "with your mother."

She shook her head as if to shake off something caught in her hair. "You, at least, must flit."

"Have you seen Sir Beichan's hounds?" said King Henry. He sat back, beneath a tapestry where hunters and hounds chased a golden stag.

Whatever the stag was, the hounds were less than Sir Beichan's. Adkyn shifted his gaze from the tapestry, fighting down his anger. He had served King Thomas well and received a fine gift. Beichan, out to seduce Lady Isobel, received finer.

"I have seen them," said Adkyn. Racing through leafless trees, their shaggy grayness against the dark trees. "And his horse as well, but—" He glanced sideways at King Henry. "I have not seen the lady he pledged to marry in foreign lands."

King Henry chuckled. "I have heard of her."

"Yet you have not seen her," said Adkyn.

King Henry's eyes narrowed. "He received fine gifts from a lord he had pleased."

He returned in the dead of winter, thought Adkyn, risking storms at sea and riding through a snowstorm. Does a man do that to leave a lord he had pleased?

Adkyn toyed with bringing word to King Thomas of the horse and hounds, and how all the land thought Beichan honored for his service, but that would take him back to those hobs. At that, Beichan spoke more gladly of his lady than of the beasts.

"Sir Beichan is the son of a great lord," said Adkyn. "His only brother is unmarried. He should carry on his line, but he betrothed himself to a woman whom no one here has seen."

"He is young, yet," said King Henry.

"He will not be so young when this lady fails to come," said Adkyn. "And who is his father's heir, if neither he nor his brother have children?" He paused as the king reflected, but King Henry did not speak; he must not know; he would not know whether Adkyn told the truth. "Perhaps—Duke Estmere."

King Henry's face froze. Adkyn glanced away to hide his face. With the threat of the duke, King Henry would not stop to consider whether Adkyn had told the truth.

"Your Majesty," said Beichan, his voice tight. Even in the room, a chilly breeze smelled of wet earth.

Seated by the window, King Henry said, gravely. "You are an heir, you will have lands. You have need of an heir of your own. Let your father rejoice to see his children's children."

His father, standing to one side, nodded.

"Your Majesty," said Beichan, "I am betrothed."

"A betrothal not fulfilled in a twelvemonth and a day is void," said King Henry. "If she exists. Who has seen her, this lady you have sworn to marry?"

Beichan's first retort, that Sir Adkyn had, did not escape him. When King Thomas had imprisoned him, Sir Adkyn had left King Thomas's service and had received a fine goshawk. Sickened, Beichan knew why King Thomas had thought Isobel in danger. If he gave Adkyn the blows he merited, King Henry would be outraged at such a treatment to his faithful subject. And he knew what Adkyn would claim if called upon.

His father shifted his weight. "Do not think that you can leave to find this lady." He bowed. "Your Majesty. I let Sir Beichan go aboard, he was a bold youth, but had I known. . . ."

"Boldness becomes the young," said King Henry. "They should not act as if gray-haired, but they are not my councilors."

Beichan felt sick again. The horn Isobel had given him would not carry across the sea.

Time, he thought. "A twelvemonth and a day. It has not been a twelvemonth and a day since—"

King Henry snorted. "A twelvemonth and a day from your return, you will wed. You can not claim that, then."

Beichan bowed deeply. It hid his face from his king and his father.

That evening, he freed his dogs. They yapped about him as he walked onto the seastrand. The dogs gamboled on the sand; Beichan looked over the waters, the swells as gray as the sky.

Softer than the wind, Beichan lamented, "I can not win to her, and she can not know to win to me."

A dog pressed its muzzle against his hand, and Beichan stroked its head. "I lamented my fate in her father's dungeon, and she came to rescue me. I don't think that lamenting now will bring news to her."

The dogs whined. The breeze ruffled their fur.

"You can not cross the sea, and the horse can not either." After a long minute, he said, "A goshawk could, but *I* did not receive a goshawk. Only Sir Adkyn did."

One dog yipped. All of them perked up.

"I can not send Sir Adkyn's goshawk, and it can not carry Lady Isobel a message—"

The dog beneath his hand barked, sharply. Dogs and a horse and a goshawk—all from a castle where the fae lived.

He looked between the dogs. "I might ask it to fly to her, and it might prove a true and gentle knight of a goshawk."

The dogs frisked again. He let his breath out. They knew the beasts of that castle better than he did. He thought of winning to the mews and freeing the bird unseen, but it could not be half the labor that Isobel had suffered to free him.

After a minute, he whistled for his dogs, and they cavorted, returning. In the kennels, where the kennel boys played at dice, the dogs licked his face, and he walked out through the stables. He looked at his horse for his excuse; it nickered at him, and he patted its neck, but his true reason was that the mews lay behind it.

"That does not," he whispered, "make it easier to get in. They will see a nobleman without a hawk entering the mews."

His horse moved its muzzle against his hand.

"If I made some excuse about seeing a bird, they would remember, and only by asking about Sir Adkyn's goshawk could I get near it—"

The horse swiveled an ear. Beichan's breath caught. "Can you speak with Sir Adkyn's goshawk, when next we go hunting?"

The horse stood so still that its tail did not twitch.

"It must fly to the Lady Isobel," Beichan said, and softly as he could, explained.

New leaves crossed, overhead, and sunlight dappled the forest floor. His horse tossed its head. Hoping, Beichan rode toward where King Henry exclaimed over Sir Adkyn's goshawk.

"Ah, Sir Beichan," called the king. "Your fine horse."

"How else might I keep pace with yours—and with Sir Adkyn's goshawk?"

The king chuckled. Sir Adkyn looked displeased. Beichan's horse nickered. The goshawk, still hooded, gave a soft cry.

Beichan had never prayed so earnestly before in his life.

"Let us see," said King Henry, "what this goshawk will bring to our table." He rode toward the meadow. Sir Adkyn followed, but Beichan slowed until he rode among the many courtiers. Ahead, the beaters struck the grass and brush, chasing out beasts. Sir Adkyn freed his bird.

The goshawk struck the air, flew higher, and circled about the field. Men muttered about how high it flew—too high for it to see to strike, little more than a dark shape against the sapphire sky.

Then it winged off. The first murmurs increased as it grew clear that the goshawk would fly from sight—toward the sea.

Across the field, Sir Adkyn eyed the crowd. His face was set in malcontent lines, and Beichan thought his gaze settled on him. Then what did it matter what a traitor thought?

Isobel walked on the ramparts, where wind blew from the sea. Her mantle billowed, and her hair flew over it.

Something crossed the waters. Not a sail. Then, she was feeding her hope, lingering here for Beichan's ship. She leaned over the stones. Slowly the shape came clear: a bird, a hawk, a goshawk.

She felt as if it had torn out her stomach, and ice had filled its place. Not *a* goshawk. *The* goshawk her father had given to Sir Adkyn.

"Why would Sir Adkyn free you?" she whispered.

It flew toward her. Stiffly, she held out her arm. The goshawk settled on it. It bore no message, tied to its leg; it only looked at her with steady eyes.

After a minute, she descended the stairs, toward the mews. She did not meet her father, which was as well. The goshawk would reveal—

Just before the bustling courtyard, in the shadows of the arched doorway, Isobel stopped. Her father might see the goshawk in the mews.

She walked into the castle.

Billy Beichan stood among the seamstresses, his clothing red among their brown and drab blue, as they gabbled about the cloth. Isobel was glad she had hid the goshawk; they would talk of other things.

"I must speak with you," she said to Billy Blind.

Seamstresses looked at her with beady bright eyes. Then they shrugged and returned to their stitches.

Isobel shut the door with care, and said, "Come." Billy Blind scuttled after. When she went toward his secret chamber, his eyes widened to the size of plates, but he said nothing.

There, the goshawk, perched on the bath tub, shifted irritably. Billy Blind studied it. Moment by moment, comprehension dawned in his face.

"Something went awry in King Henry's land," said Isobel.

"Not here, not here." Billy Blind bowed deeply to the goshawk. "Our gracious messenger is entitled to rest. I will bring him a brace of rabbits for his dinner, and partridges in the morning, before his return."

Isobel swallowed. She did not know if the castle held another such secret place. But the goshawk looked at her with one golden eye, and she swallowed again. Perhaps the goshawk did not realize that it had been bestowed for treachery.

They stole down the corridor. The goshawk settled behind them. Isobel whispered, "Something is wrong. I must learn—"

Billy Blind said, "Sir Beichan is a bold young knight. I would think him more likely to guess he could bring you home in a year and in truth need three, than to guess three years, and in truth need one."

Isobel's hands spread. "Sir Adkyn came from there, too, and his goshawk flew back here. Something went awry, and Sir Adkyn is not the only one who could have suffered. I must know what it is."

"Well, if it can be learned—"

"Can be or can not be," said Isobel, "it must be."

Billy Blind's mouth twisted further than a human's mouth could. "My lady, what would you *do*?"

She felt a fool, but she had pledged her word. "Cross the sea to him, if need be."

"And you are certain you could reach him in time?"

Isobel let her breath out. "If by no other means—I would be in *great* need, would I not?" When Billy Blind did not speak, she hardened her voice. "I would be."

Only such daylight as came through the door lit the hut. The scent of dried herbs mixed with the dust, and the old woman sat on her stool before a fireplace holding only ash. Her hood shadowed her face; Adkyn could make out only a hint of her wrinkles.

"A potion of forgetfulness?" said the woman.

"You will serve the king in this."

She laughed. "A king's gratitude, Sir Knight? *I* do nothing for that price."

"I do not expect you to," said Adkyn. Who but Sir Beichan would have frightened off his goshawk? His horse and hounds were not enough, beside that fine goshawk. King Henry and his court might exclaim over the goshawk's return, but he would not suffer this treatment. King Henry would forbid a direct attack, but many maidens, and their mothers, would gladly receive his aid. "I have coin."

"Humm." She rocked on her stool. "To forget, to forget, a posset that would fog days, months, years."

Adkyn started. Forgetting everything would show that Sir Beichan was bewitched. "Not that much. Only a woman he fancies, whom he will never see again."

She shifted. "To forget a woman, and her alone—to remember all else—if he does not see her again, ever, perhaps. He lays eyes on her—"

"He will never lay eyes on her again," said Adkyn.

Lady Blanche embroidered and spoke with her daughter, Lady Elspeth, who might might be pretty if she looked less cowed.

Beichan looked at the game of draughts his father played with Lord William, Elspeth's father.

Minutes later, Lady Elspeth offered him a golden cup. It would be discourteous to refuse; Beichan drank. The wine held an odd, bitter taste. As he lowered it, Elspeth smiled, tentatively.

He thought he had forgotten something. His tongue touched his lips. Something about a twelvemonth and a day.

In the garden, the warm breezes smelled of roses.

"We have no reason to put off the wedding," said Lord William. "Once the banns of marriage are read, the man and woman should swiftly enjoy one another as husband and wife."

"I can't," said Beichan. "It has not been a twelvemonth and a day."

"A twelvemonth and a day from what? You agree that marriage is prudent, and Lady Elspeth, suitable. Yet you insist on a twelvemonth and a day!"

Beichan breathed in and out. With careless glee, a bird sang. A bumblebee wandered between flowers. Roses nodded. As if all the world wished him to yield—

"A twelvemonth and a day," said Beichan. "I gave my word." His mouth set. He remembered saying that, if he did not remember when he had given it.

Lord William opened his mouth as if to threaten to withhold his daughter. Beichan looked coldly back at him.

Lord William muttered under his breath and left. Beichan watched him go. Perhaps his own father would return, or Lady Blanche. Elspeth herself had not begged. She might yet.

But the postern gate stood near here.

He went with some stealth, but he saddled his horse and freed his dogs. With the dogs yipping, he rode into the woods. His horse and his hounds, brought back from foreign lands.

"You were gifts to me," he said. "But whose?"

Leaves rustled. The horse tossed its head, and the hounds whined. He wished he could ride away.

But the twelvemonth and a day would soon be up.

Isobel yawned.

Billy Blind's whisper pierced the hangings. "Wake *up*, my lady!"

She blinked and sat up. Billy Blind pulled apart the curtains at the foot of her bed; he stood on a stool there.

"Wake up. How can you *sleep* on Beichan's wedding day?"

"Wed—" Isobel stared.

"Bring two of your ladies. Dress them well—dress yourself well—and come to the shore."

Herself dressed in scarlet, Marguerite and Jeanne behind her in green, Isobel watched the gray swells of the waves. The air was cold; she was lucky it did not snow, yet.

"My lady!" said Jeanne. "These belts have gold enough—we can not stand here where any robber—"

The ship sailed about the promontory. In the sudden silence, Isobel let her breath out. Ivory and silk gleamed in the dawn light.

A small figure, in red, stood by the wheel. "Come aboard, my lady," called Billy Blind. "I will be your steersman!"

"Thanks be to God!" She walked over the sands.

"My lady!" said Jeanne. "You can not go on that!"

Isobel walked on, without looking back. Breezes pulled at her skirt. "You do not have to come."

Marguerite said sharply, "She can not go unattended."

Isobel smiled. Loyal servants, she thought. Billy Blind threw a gleaming anchor overboard and ran out a gangplank. Her ladies ran after her.

"Do not look down-hearted," said Billy Blind. "Remember that the ceremony is invalid! You are his betrothed."

"I would rather," said Isobel, "arrive before the wedding night. A marriage can also be set aside because it was not consummated."

Billy Blind roared with laughter. "Still, we must bide a bit."

She scowled, but as she opened her mouth, something moved on the beach. She blinked. Skipping over the sands came lasses the shade of driftwood, wearing blue gowns, and with their gaze on the gangplank. Behind them came lumbering great limbed goblins, whom she had often seen while they cut firewood, and lugged water, and swarms of hobs, not carrying sewing or laundry or pots, or any other of their tasks.

Her breath gushed out.

"We'd've managed, somehow, if you left with your husband and your father's blessing," said Billy Blind. "Some to go and some to stay. But since you are leaving in secret, against your father's will, and he had moved against your betrothed. . . ." He shrugged.

She turned her gaze back to the shore. Rank after rank of fae skipped or scampered or plodded toward the ship.

They filed onto the ship neatly enough, and went below decks—far more of them than should have fit—laughing and chattering all the way.

Finally, last of all, ogres and spriggans clomped across the sands.

"And what brings you here?" said Isobel, her voice ringing over the waters. "Do you really wish to serve my lord husband?"

They hesitated, and then began to inch forward.

Billy Blind's eyes rolled up, and he contemplated the sky. "They have to, you know, my lady. They were loyal to your mother and now to you. . . ."

Isobel's mouth tightened.

"They will obey you," he said. "And him."

After a moment, she nodded.

Grinning again, Billy Blind hauled up the anchor, and went to the wheel. Isobel went to the bow. Wind carried her skirts and her hair forward with it.

King Henry came himself to grace the wedding of Lord Beichan and Lady Elspeth.

Beichan contemplated the dishes. Musicians played, guests laughed, and from the jerky movements of her hand, Elspeth felt the honor as much as he did. She should drink more wine; it might put color in her cheeks.

The sea breezes stirred banners. By the door, voices rose, but the porter came in and dropped to one knee.

"Sire!" he called. "Lord Beichan! A lady at the door begs to speak with you—with the bridegroom."

Angry mutters stirred the hall, his own father glowered, but no one else spoke.

The porter shook his head in wonderment. "I have never seen such a lady. Nor even a lady such as the two who attend her, all in green, and she in scarlet."

Lady Blanche rose, glittering with gold. "If they are brave without, we are brave within—you could have excepted our bride, and one or two of our company."

Despite himself, Beichan felt his mouth twitch. He did not doubt who else Lady Blanche thought should be excepted.

"Never, my lady," said the porter. "These ladies wear gold in their belt, each enough to buy an earldom—and young Sir Beichan's hounds from across the sea, they fawned on her—"

Beichan slapped down his cup.

"Is it the custom of your house," said Lady Blanche, "to wed your bride in the morning, and abandon her in the evening?"

Lady Blanche, thought Beichan, knew something. "Your daughter can go home none the worse for me—she has received only a kiss on her mouth, and can take her dowry with her."

He did not wait to hear her response.

Wind pulled at her hair, at her skirt, at the fur of the dogs. Sometimes, it carried music; sometimes, voices—

She was a fool. If Beichan had forgotten his promise, what could she do? Drag him to the altar?

A young man came down the stairs. Beichan, a bridegroom arrayed in scarlet and gold, as handsome as she remembered him. Her breath came out raggedly. His face was clouded.

Then he looked at her, and the clouds vanished. The dogs yipped. Beichan walked by them, to take her in his arms and kiss her.

Great cheers rouse up from the sea below. Long moments later, Isobel drew back from Beichan's embrace, to see all the fae rejoicing, some swinging from the masts and sheets of the ship as they waved caps in the air, some frolicking on the deck, and all about the castle, people gaped and stared.

Except Sir Adkyn. Who looked bitter and ill-used.

She smiled radiantly on him.

Jewel of the Tiger

The path rose steadily up the mountain, with steep rock and grass to either side. Jyron glanced back. In the valleys below, the windbreaks, great earthen mounds, and the canals looked strong, but they would not have taken this trek if they were strong enough.

Milas's hand gripped his arm like a claw. "Stop dreaming. There's the wizard's house." He jerked his head. It looked like a cottage, or half of one, but it was built into the mountain. Milas shook his arm. "We brought you to help on the trail—you don't need brains for that. Not to talk. *We* will talk with the wizard."

Bizal, his hands on his hips, said, "This is too important to be bungled. Without crops, we will all beg in the cities."

Jyron pulled his arm away. He had not come for pleasure. They walked on, and he followed, lagging, but not so far that he did not see the door open.

The wizard stood on the cottage's threshold. His face was as brown and wrinkled as sun-baked earth, and his white hair and beard foamed like starlight about his face and over his ivory robes. Jyron's tongue touched his lips. The wizard's dark eyes, looking from face to face, glittered like water deep in the well.

Milas and Bizal stuttered out their message: their valley perished for the want of work on the canals and the windbreaks, and the king would not maintain them. What would it cost to have the work done by magic? They glanced at each other when words failed them.

They had sounded confident in the village.

They stammered into silence. The wizard looked between them, and then to Jyron, and back to the two before him. "For such a spell, I will cast—and will cast it only—in return for the jewel of the tiger."

Milas and Bizal gave the wizard's cottage baneful glances until the mountainside hid it from sight. Jyron kept his gaze on the footing and tried to think. Halfway down, perhaps out of earshot, Milas burst out, "The jewel of the tiger? What on earth did he mean by that? Why doesn't he just conjure it himself? Or at least *tell us* what he meant."

Jyron looked up. "He—"

"There's the library," said Bizal. The first trees appeared ahead of them, the first land where the hills gave enough shelter from wind. Bizal glared at them. "If the wizard has to live so far from it to make it difficult for us to reach him, it might make it difficult for him to reach things, too."

Milas brightened. "Something so impressive that it would repay a wizard for his work on our land—such a thing could not be an *obscure* piece of lore."

"We must do *something*," said Bizal. "We need the windbreaks. We need the pools and streams."

Jyron remembered how the crops had withered. If their last year had not been wet, they could not even have sent the three of them in search of an escape. Bizal told the truth.

"And we can not afford to do the work by hand. That would take longer than discovering what this Jewel of the Tiger is."

"The library it will have to be," said Milas.

"But—" said Jyron.

"Oh, be still," said Bizal.

Jyron glared at them. If the wizard had asked for the flower of a rosebush, they might have guessed. Why did it have to be some strange and marvelous thing? The jungle—closer than the city— might have marvelous ruins in it, but it also had tigers. And roads. Tigers killed men, and men carried jewels. Once the tiger had such jewels in its lair, whose would be? No one else's but the tiger's.

His eyes narrowed. Of course, if he *showed* them, it wouldn't matter if they didn't listen. Better even. If they listened, they could claim the credit. If he showed them, they would find out too late.

He smiled, a little.

The open door left the small house still dim, but he needed only a little light. He slid more bread into the pack. Too much would burden him, he did not have as long a journey as Bizal and Milas, off to the city, and besides, the pack was full. Jyron slung the pack on.

"Jyron!" called Lisiza, waving from the cook fire. "I made a special batch of sweets tonight."

Lisiza's sweets were not lightly to be missed—but they could not be half so sweet as the look on Bizal and Milas's faces, when they returned to find someone else had taken the place of hero. "I'll come before they're all eaten."

Birds chattered in the trees. Jyron peered about. The layer upon layer of leaves shadowed the entire forest, coloring every scrap of light with green, but he *thought* it grew dimmer because sunset came.

Jyron rubbed his eyes. A rock ridge stood in the midst of the trees; he had seen it before he descended into the valley that sheltered the jungle. He could sleep there. He walked on, over the forest floor where leaves lay centuries deep, and through tangles of ferns and vines. When a rock stood, uncovered, to the right of his path, he looked at it warily and gauged his directions to ensure he did not go astray.

But the rock proved a harbinger. Soon Jyron climbed a slope of rocks. Without the trees, ferns and vines grew even more thickly, but even at evening, sunlight touched him in mote-laden beams. For all their rough surfaces, the rocks made stepping stones, easier to walk on than the greenery. By the ruby-red light, he leapt from rock to rock. He stopped on one boulder, surrounded by vines and dead branches.

Something hissed.

Jyron jerked back. The snake slithered from its shadowed rest: dark in the sunset light, thicker than Jyron's arm. Its mouth gaped. Poison glittered on its fangs, and Jyron drew back again. Go away, snake, he thought, I'm too big to swallow, I have nothing against you—I have nothing against the tiger, even, since it doesn't want its jewels.

The snake slithered closer. Drawing his dagger, Jyron inched back, and his foot landed on a branch. The dead wood splintered instantly, wood soft with rot went flying, Jyron's foot fell into a crevice, and he fell, sprawling.

Aching, fighting for breath, Jyron looked about. After a dazed moment, he saw his dagger glitter, flat against the stone. The snake hissed. Jyron did not try to rise but eased his hand toward the blade.

The snake lunged, but not toward him. Its body covered the blade. Then it slithered about it, an intricate pattern, always about the dagger. Jyron stared, blankly. He should have gotten a second dagger before he left, somehow—however little he had in way of grudges against anyone. His hand clenched into a fist, and he watched the snake. Except Milas and Bizal, and *them* he only wanted to show up.

"I don't even want to show *you* up, snake," he muttered.

The snake hissed as if it understood, and would dispute the point. It coiled, readying itself to spring. Jyron leapt to snatch the dagger by the point, whirl it about, and slice off the snake's head. Poison splattered. Jyron leapt back, but the drops still sprayed on dagger and cloth as well as stone.

Jyron gave the dagger a long glance, trying to be glad that the poison had only touched the blade, before climbing back two stones, where moss grew. He thrust the blade into it, cleaning off blood and poison. The spots on his tunic looked even darker, though the light faded. He pulled the tunic out and sliced off the affected cloth before climbing back up the ridge. He could hear Amara now, about the waste of cloth, as if women spun and wove and sewed for their own amusement.

At the height of the ridge, he looked into the valley, dark with evening and greenery. Once he got the jewel, and the wizard cast his spells, Amara could tell him as long as she had breath.

Only a fool would venture toward the tiger's lair at night. But he spent a long time climbing over rocks, looking for any beast laired in the nooks, before he lay down to sleep. Frogs started to call, and Jyron stirred restlessly. If they continued all night—he sighed.

The frogs continued, and other noises, less identifiable, joined them. He shifted. Stones made a hard bed.

The birds' chorus had replaced the frogs', and sounded even more loudly. Jyron stretched into the cold air and winced. He hoped the tiger laired deep in the valley.

He rose to his feet slowly, but moving was the best way to recover. Jyron clambered to his feet and started down the slope. Greenery encroached on the rocks. Vines with bell-like flowers surrounded him, each gaudy bloom as large as his head. He eyed them warily. If the valley produced such monster flowers, what else could it produce? Old women told children stories of a city in this jungle.

He looked back to the stones. The quicker he left, the less it mattered. The stones were easier to walk on, as easy as a stair—and then he glanced back up the stones. They looked like a stair.

He shivered.

The birds' singing sank with day, but calls still rang. Every now and again, a bird swooped through the hanging vines. Jyron eased his way through the gloom. A bird sprang, squawking, from a bush before him. He grimaced as its red feathers vanished back into the leaves. If the tiger had been near—he was not hunting, he reminded himself. He had no need to kill the tiger.

It would make Milas and Bizal look even more like fools, suggested a mischievous thought.

Jyron smiled, but he had brought no spears. Only a fool would kill a tiger with a dagger. And paying the wizard, thus saving the valley, made even a tiger-slaying look petty. He eased his way forward. The tiger would not even miss the jewels he would take. He kept his gaze on the forest floor, looking for any sign of tiger feet. Not even the great deer of the forest would leave tracks as large.

Water gurgled ahead. Jyron drew his breath. He himself had awaited prey at water, but now, some beast might await *him*. He drew his dagger and peered through the greenery; something moved by the water, and he froze, but a moment's glance showed monkeys sat on the stream bank, and among the trees. Jyron strode forward before another beast came. Screaming and scolding, the monkeys leapt away. He forded the stream quickly and, though the monkeys went on screaming, cast about, eyeing tracks where they welled with water. It did not take long before he could know that the tiger had drunk from this stream. He crouched to measure the prints with his hand. It was a good thing he had not come to hunt this beast, spear or no spear, but he began to backtrack it.

The monkeys' clamor faded into the distance. The leaves and drier earth could not keep him from seeing the tiger tracks.

A snake hissed at him. He looked frantically about. A small brown snake, not poisonous, wriggled off. Jyron still had to fight to get his breath back, before he plugged on. The tracks increased. They could not have been lain down in one day; the tiger's lair was near. Jyron fought to breathe deeply. If the tiger rested there now, he would hide until it left.

The greenery about the lair was more beaten down. Three dead trees had smashed out their way through the jungle. Bones were visible, too many bones to mean anything but that the killer dragged meat to its lair to devour. Some bones he dismissed at once, as deer or pig. Others looked human, and some were fresh.

He saw no sign of the tiger. Best to be in and out before it returned, then. Trying to pretend they were not human, he sifted through the bones. He found scraps of cloth and bits of leather. Now and again, he found a rusted knife, or a tarnished ring, or an old coin—no jewels, just such goods as the poor might carry.

He thought of Milas and Bizal, but their scorn did not quell the prickling in his back. He bit his lip and remembered how the crops withered. They needed water and protection from the wind. He would show those two that *he* could provide it.

He looked about again. By a dead tree, something glittered. He stood to walk over.

A snarl erupted behind him, and he felt the air move. Almost before he felt it, he threw himself sideways. A claw still struck his back, racking fire. Jyron found himself lying on the dead leaves, staring at an enraged tiger, his back wet with blood.

He snatched his dagger and braced himself. The tiger lunged again, and he struck, his dagger going deep into the fur, drawing blood. The dagger would staunch most of the flow, he knew, and pulled on the hilt. The dagger came out, a little, and he saw blood, but the hilt slid from his fingers. The tiger reared up, bearing the dagger from his reach. It came down again, and Jyron rolled away, over ferns and branches, and near one of the fallen trees. He snatched at some dead wood, found one stick that seemed both sound and pointed, and whirled on the tiger.

It left a trail of blood as it stalked him, but not so much as he left. Even if the dagger wound weakened it, even if it died, he would leave his bones here first. The tiger, growling, paced forward. His back ached. Then, he could bandage the wounds, more or less, if he could only—he glanced at the dead trees, half fallen, and scrambled. The tiger roared, but Jyron dived into the cramped area beneath a deadfall, a place too small for the tiger.

A twig prodded his back, and other twigs his arms and legs, but better twigs than teeth. He glanced back, to see if the tiger kept watch.

It did.

But a moment later, it started to pace. It shook its head very oddly.

His heart pounded in his chest, so hard that it shook him.

The tiger tossed its head, and it moved far more slowly. Almost stumbling.

Jyron's breath hissed out. The snake's venom had splattered the blade. His heart hammered with hope.

The pain might madden the tiger. It might attack more fiercely than before, and have no heed for the branches or its own safety. But his thoughts did not calm his heart.

Long minutes later, the tiger collapsed.

Jyron slowly let his breath out. He pushed against the branches, making them shift. The tiger did not stir. He crept out. Its eyes opened, but its paws did not even twitch.

His own wounds no longer bled, though they still hurt.

Keeping a wary eye on the tiger, Jyron rummaged through the bones and dead leaves beneath the dead tree. He found gemstones—tiger's eyes, and only the aches and the tiger lying on the forest floor kept him from laughing—but if the wizard wanted a jewel in truth, he did not want to return to this forest.

If he brought back a cheap stone, which failed, and he did not return to the lair for another jewel for fear of the snakes, Milas and Bizal would laugh at his folly.

That thought smarted, but his hands moved only a little more swiftly. It did not smart more than his wounds.

And then he settled on a red stone. A ruby, he thought. Perhaps a garnet, but faceted and clear. The wizard could not say that this was not a jewel.

The tiger tried to roar. The sound was weak but clear. Jyron, giving it a wary glance, saw that the dagger was no longer in the wound.

Birds sang.

Jyron remembered the snake.

Slowly, very slowly, he edged across the clearing and bent down, with both eyes watching the tiger, to feel for the dagger. It had been poisoned, he reminded himself, and glanced down quickly to ensure that he seized the hilt.

The tiger snarled.

He eased away and into the forest, keeping his gaze on the tiger. Only when his ankles banged into deadwood did he turn and flee.

Bird cries echoed the air. Monkeys screamed. He wished he could run, but he would trip, and he was not certain that his feet would obey him. He hurried as best he could; after a time, that meant he trudged along.

The slope started to rise, and he slowed. He felt hot. Feverish? he wondered, and stopped dead in his tracks. For a moment, he swayed, but if he fell here—he plodded on.

As he climbed on the rocks, the evening's breezes were cool, and the sunset glowed with color: far more radiant than the jewel, scarlet and flame and gold, with violet about the edges, on feathery clouds.

For a moment, he saw wings, and even wings beating the air.

He blinked. He had felt feverish. . . . There were only feathery clouds, and the moon beginning to rise. It shone dull orange now, like a bonfire in the distance, but it would be full when it had risen. He could walk by it.

He turned to descend into the next valley, and heard a raptor's scream.

He spun about, staggered, and crouched, fumbling with his dagger. A great eagle was outlined against the sunset, like a dire shadow, but he could feel the wind from its wing beats, and its claws and beak came down upon him. His left arm rose, without his quite willing it, to shield his face.

He managed to free his dagger as the claws bit into his left arm, but he struck only its feathers and it wheeled off, screaming again as three feathers fell to the earth.

He panted for breath. His arm stung and dripped blood. He glanced about, saw the eagle whirling in the air, and scrambled for a rock, to put his back to it. He had barely reached it before the eagle plunged again.

This time his dagger struck its wing, and the eagle splattered blood on the stone as it flew away. The evening breezes were chill, but he stood, panting hard, to ensure that it did not attack again.

He could not see it.

For a long minute, Jyron strained his ears, but no birds or monkeys protested its intrusion. He swallowed. He had thought he was growing feverish.

He could walk as well as stand while feverish, he told himself, but that did not inspire his feet.

Milas and Bizal would laugh their heads off at him, even if the jewel proved to be the jewel of the tiger, and he succeeded. To linger in the forest, in peril—but that thought did not inspire him.

"Why did we go to see the wizard anyway?"

His voice was flat in his dejection. Still, to utter the words aloud summoned up memories, of dry fields and hungry children. He staggered on.

The path to the wizard's house stood before him. Jyron wavered. He could go to the village, assure them that he had the jewel, and get an escort there. It would not make the way much safer, he already knew that no bandits lurked along the road, but he would have witnesses to his deed.

But the windbreaks would not be built as swiftly.

He trudged up the slope.

The wizard stood at the doorway to scowl at him. "One of you alone? The only one fool enough to disbelieve me? I want no dealings with you without the jewel of the tiger."

Jyron rummaged in his pouch and brought out the jewel. Ruby or garnet, it flashed red in the sunlight.

The wizard's eyes flashed brighter. He snatched the jewel and held it up. It glinted, and he began to shout.

The earth rippled under Jyron's feet, bearing him away. He shouted and threw out his arms to steady himself, but the ripple did not cease—and he did not fall, but was swept down, into his own valley, where people ran and shouted.

Earth shifted. It rose from itself, at the end of their fields. . . .

Lisiza shouted, "Jyron! What's happening?"

"The wizard's windbreaks," shouted Jyron. "I found the price!"

Even with the earth shifting, gazes turned him.

There were worse things than convalescence.

Jyron lay, propped up in bed, and drank the honey-sweetened brew. Outside the doorway, the children cavorted. They were already flourishing—as the greenery was, about them.

Amara's sweet voice caroled outside the cottage. "You should have seen it!"

"We," said Milas, "didn't find a thing. . . ."

"It's just as well that Jyron did, then, isn't it?"

For a moment, Jyron thought of rising, and seeing the look on Milas's face, or Bizal's. But the children were still playing, and he wanted to watch that more.

Also by Mary Catelli

Curses And Wonders
Dragon Slayer
Eyes of the Sorceress
Fever and Snow
Mermaids' Song
Sword and Shadow
The Book of Bone
Witch-Prince Ways
Dragonfire and Time
Enchantments And Dragons
Jewel of the Tiger
Over the Sea, To Me
The Dragon's Cottage
The Maze, the Manor, and the Unicorn
The White Menagerie
A Diabolical Bargain
Madeleine and the Mists
Magic And Secrets
The Lion and the Library
The Princess Goes Into The Forest
The Wolf and the Ward
The Witch-Child and the Scarlet Fleet
Treachery And Spells
Winter's Curse
Crow Curse
Free Passage
Isabelle and the Siren
Journeys And Wizardry
Lifestone

Magic of the Lost God
Never Comment On A Likeness
One Name
The Drunken Mermaids
The Turtle in the Sea of Sand
Were I You
Where There Is Smoke

www.ingramcontent.com/pod-product-compliance
Lightning Source LLC
Chambersburg PA
CBHW030302130626
46549CB00002B/651